THE DARKLY STEWART MYSTERIES

The Woman Who Tasted Death

D G Wood

Copyright © 2015 D G Wood
All rights reserved.

www.darklystewart.com

ISBN: 1517488265
ISBN 13: 9781517488260

"DG Wood has crafted an addictive heroine you can't get enough of. Darkly Stewart lives in the shadows of our fears and haunts our senses.
She's the most original character in years; an investigator who discovers her own past holds the key to the ultimate mystery.
Darkly shines a light on horror that we've never seen. Reader beware, you'll never think about the woods the same way again."
— **Gary Grossman, Bestselling Author of the EXECUTIVE series and OLD EARTH.**

"DG Wood has written a really strong, well-rounded FEMALE lead... which is brilliant. The novel took me on a journey I didn't want to put down.
There's enough intrigue for the well-read, and enough prediction for the DaVinci demon lovers out there. A happy mix to appeal to all."
—*Jamie MacLachlan, Actor on EASTENDERS, WAKING THE DEAD.*

"As someone who grew up with the classic gothics, I resent the way my beloved horror legends are being reinterpreted to make them romantic for today's teenage audiences, so I was drawn to DG Wood's new, yet respectful, take on werewolves. He has set up a plot with characters who can populate a series and who have enough of a past to keep the present interesting. This is both a cinematic and literary work, revealing details as they are needed and supplying a mature richness of character. It's also creepy as hell."

— *Nat Segaloff, Film Producer & Author of MR. HUSTON/MR. NORTH: LIFE, DEATH, AND MAKING JOHN HUSTON'S LAST FILM.*

ACKNOWLEDGMENTS

There are a number of people who have been instrumental in helping me breathe life into Darkly. My wife, Wendy, has displayed great patience and confidence in the promises of tomorrow. My manager, Lorraine, encourages me to think big on every endeavour. Gary Grossman, the American novelist, has advised me as both mentor and friend that if I am to write a series of novels, I need to just write those novels. Don't delay, get it done. I'm getting it done, Gary. I am grateful to Rufus and The Camera House for providing my artistic spirit with a tangible home. And how many people would an author touch without the right editor? Thank you, Felisha Baquera.

Most of all, I have my daughter, Audrey, to thank. Her impending arrival necessitated a flurry of creative work, laying the foundations for a new Darkly world to come. Parents often speak of giving their child a push to take chances. Before leaving the womb, my daughter inspired me to leave the collaborative comfort of the television writing room to begin a journey that is an invention purely of my own imagination. She's the best thing I've ever done with my life, and I have no doubt that the courage RCMP Constable Darkly Stewart displays in desperate times foreshadows what my daughter is to become.

Finally, thank you to the following individuals, who gave their support at the time of Darkly's inception: Jennifer Wood, Grahame Barry Wood, Kim Wood, Denise Wood, David & Jenny Flood, Graydon James, Jennie Grimes, KJ Miller, Michael Rawlins, Alexander Campbell, Luanne Fp, Francis Testa, Ione Butler, Todd Witham, Jamie Maclachlan, Kathleen Dimpfl and Julie Harter, Constance Boyd, Sandra Wilson, Ashley Buckwell, Christopher Bruton, Janet Pomerantz, Lindsey Zipkin, Jon Finck, Jason Chesworth and Tricia Wettlaufer.

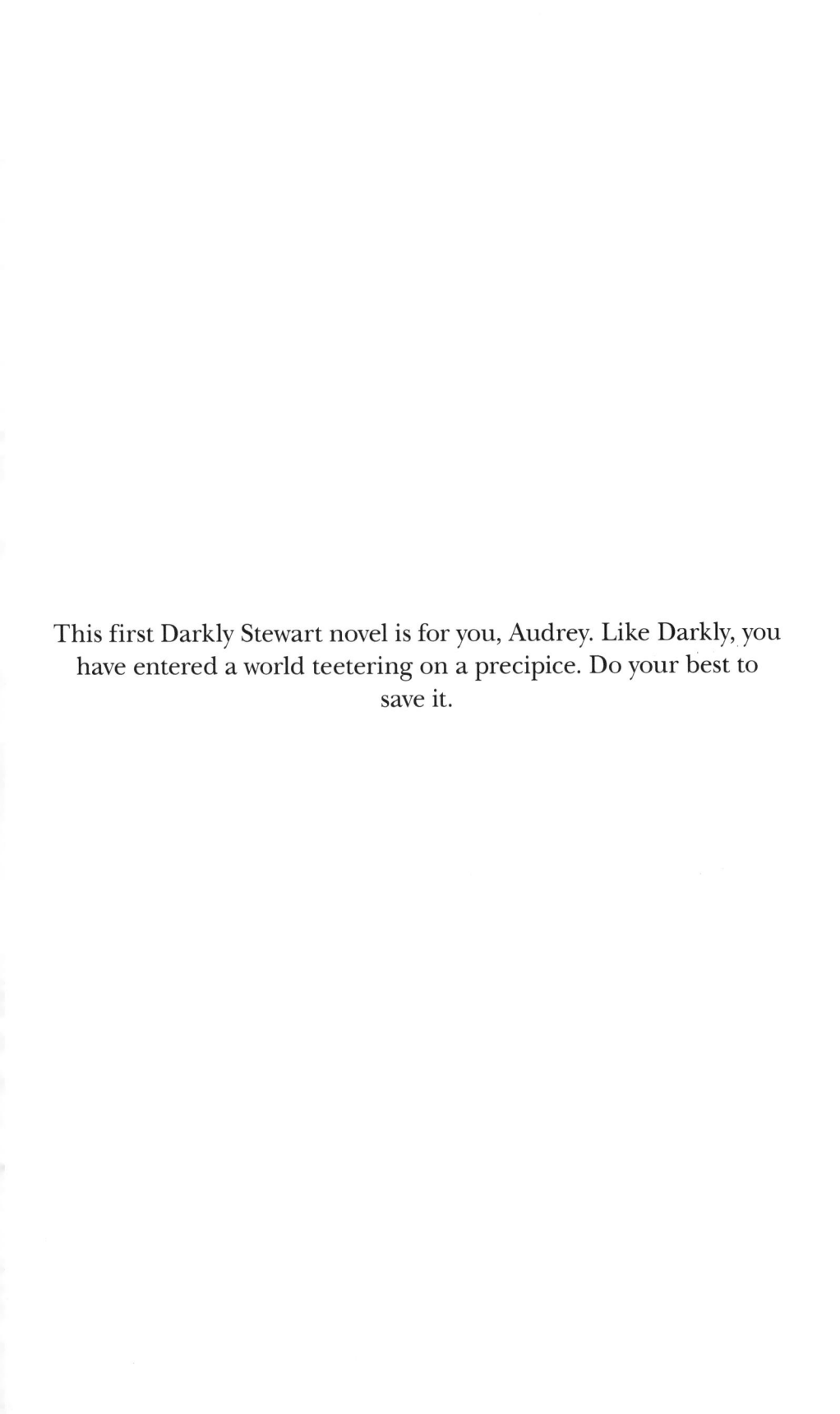

This first Darkly Stewart novel is for you, Audrey. Like Darkly, you have entered a world teetering on a precipice. Do your best to save it.

"Every monster was a man first." – *Edward Albee*

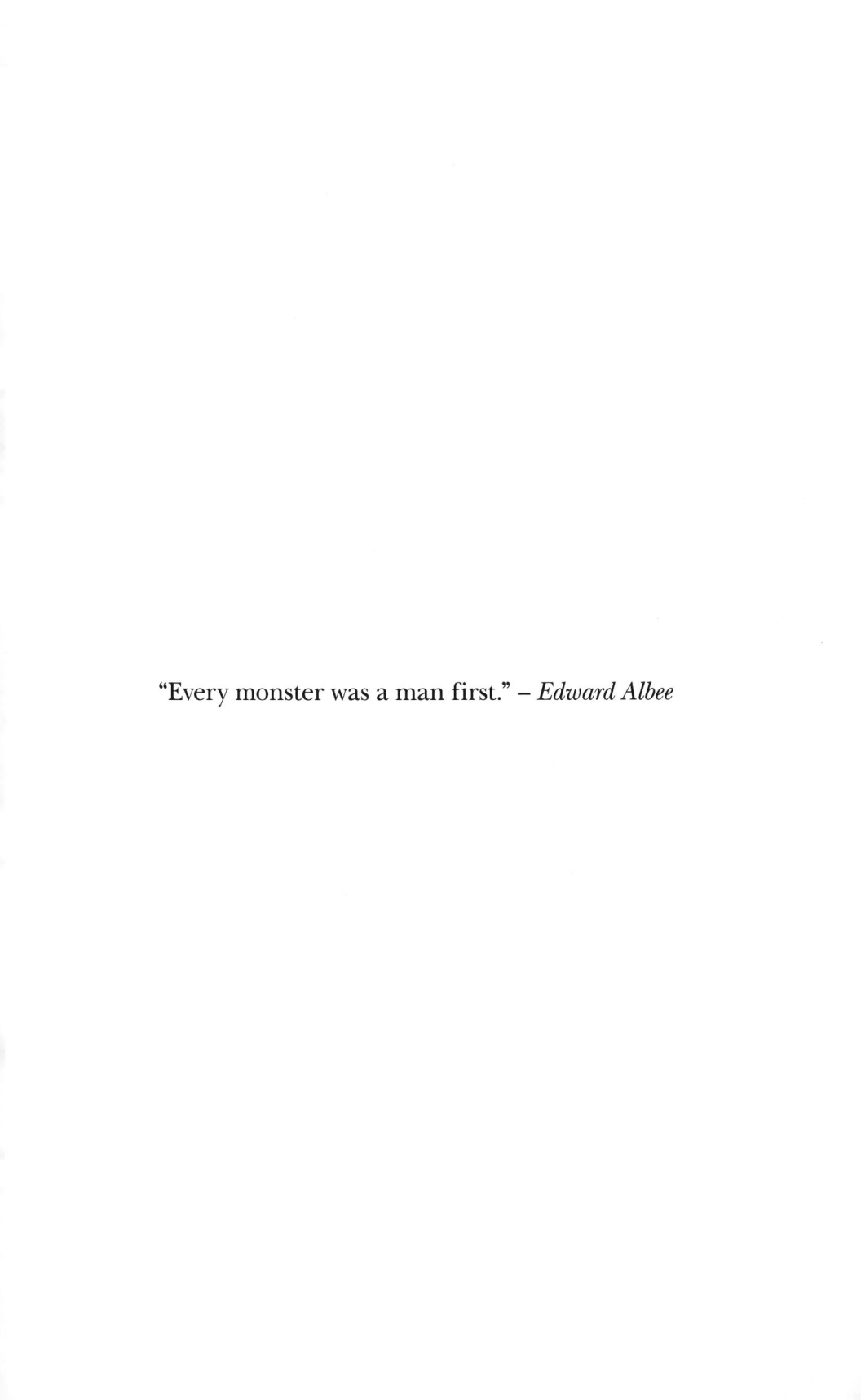

PROLOGUE

All parents share core traits in common. Each couple dives blindly into the spirit of the messy miracle that is childbirth and spends the next eighteen years praying that what they push out of the nest will become something better than their own humble hopes and dreams. Dreams that one day seemed grand in their own right, now pale next to the god-like power to recreate oneself in flesh and baby powder. Not just a new beginning, but a new soul.

Worldly-unaware jocks and small-town beauty queens can cook up a kinder, more generous, nobler copy of themselves, and cutting right to the chase, a more profitable version of mummy and daddy.

Darkly Stewart was greeted with the same affirmation every morning at the breakfast table: "You can become anything you want to be." How would Darkly's biological parents have reacted had they known then that she would grow up to become a cop?

Considering Darkly's unfortunate birthright, they likely would have been grateful to see her survive to adulthood without incident.

With family road-trips, comes the expectation that a child will entertain herself while the adults keep their eyes on the road. So it was with Darkly during the long drive up the Pacific coast, across the Cascade Mountains and into British Columbia. She didn't mind. She was only seven years old, but already an introspective, private human being. Fifty-four hours of driving and five completed crossword books later, she had the vocabulary of a child twice her age.

Not neglecting the coolness factor of personal growth, her CD collection was filled with the likes of the Beatles and Nirvana. She had endured her fair share of classical music, too, while still in the womb. As far back as she could remember, she would break into the spontaneous humming of Beethoven's Ode to Joy, with no clue as to where she had heard it before. This affectation pleased Darkly's mother greatly, who wanted her daughter to experience everything her own isolated childhood had denied her.

As Darkly now listened to *Let It Be* on her CD Walkman and searched her mind for a four-letter word beginning with 's' that means desist, her mother, Catharine, yelled out, "Stop!" Such a simple word. One of the first we learn as a child. Rarely does it bring to a halt only what is intended.

Jack slammed on the brakes.

"What?!" he yelled, as a cola can went flying from the cup holder, spilling over the carpet. "Damn. Great. There goes the frigging discount."

"Sorry. We passed it, Jack."

Catharine scanned the map draped over the dash with her fingertip, as Jack mopped up the sugary soda with an entire pack of travel tissue.

"It's the last dirt road on the right before the sign. You know, I could drive, and you could navigate. If you want."

Jack ignored the suggestion.

"Darkly, honey, throw this away for Daddy."

Jack passed the dripping clump of tissue over his shoulder.

Darkly left her perch on her swivel bucket-seat to grudgingly accept the dripping mess.

"Gross," Darkly said as she held the clump at arm's length until releasing the tissue into a plastic grocery bag hanging off a cupboard in the RV's kitchenette. She wiped her hands on her jeans.

Catharine removed a kerchief printed with the US flag from her head. Jack accepted it and softened as he dried his hands with it. He smiled and said, "I hope no one sees. They could get me for treason."

There again was the light-hearted hippy Catharine had fallen in love with and the man who accepted her despite her one big flaw.

Darkly's hair was the same color her mother's used to be before the gray: jet black. It even had those silver sparkles in the right light. It suited her mother's maiden name. When it came time to consider baby names, modern options of Brittany, Tabatha, and Holly were abandoned to combine her mother's last name with her father's. Besides the mop of coal on her head, Darkly was born with a light down of dark hair on her arms and legs. Thankfully, it fell out in the weeks after birth.

Outside the RV window, on the side of the road, a weather-worn, wooden sign proclaimed "Town of Wolf Woods, Population 284." They were close.

"You don't want to head into town first?" Jack asked his wife. "Burger and a local brew?"

"That's not funny, Jack. I'm getting a migraine. I just want to take it easy tonight. Tomato soup, grilled cheese, and french fries, hun?" Catharine called out to Darkly.

"Mmmmm. My favorite."

Truth is, Darkly ate nothing else. Catharine occasionally hid chunks of tuna under a quarter pound of melted cheddar, in an attempt to force her daughter to consume more of what was good for her. Like any good mother, the fries were always baked, never fried.

"You're the boss."

Jack resigned himself to family card night in the RV.

"You know I hate it when you say that."

Catharine's migraine was quickly getting worse.

"Sorry."

Jack put the RV into reverse, and as the Wolf Woods sign grew smaller, Darkly squished it between her forefinger and thumb. Jack stopped, shifted the RV back into drive, and turned onto the missed dirt and gravel road leading off the highway.

"Everyone hold on. It's gonna get bumpy." Jack turned to his wife and asked, "How long?"

Catharine put her finger on the map's distance key, then on the red line that marked the rural road on the map. She measured the distance to the symbol of a small car inside a mountain peak.

"Looks like the outlook's maybe 5 miles."

Catharine stared out the window, immediately transported a far greater distance.

Jack reached over and squeezed his wife's hand.

"It's going to be alright. You'll see."

Catharine's return home would not be put off any longer. It would also be the greatest gift she could ever give her extended family, ending centuries of affliction. Darkly was the proof of cure she would show them.

The RV wound its way deep into the forest of birch, poplar, and maple, giving Darkly that giddy feeling of her stomach in free-fall as the road became a roller-coaster of steep inclines and sharp descents.

The woods here were so thick and close together, she could only focus on objects ten or so feet into the forest. A bear could be a few feet beyond that, tracking her, and she would never know. That was Darkly's greatest hope for the family getaway: to see a bear. And no, zoos didn't count.

On the outskirts of Seattle, the family had waited all night at a town dump. They sat there glued to the windshield, the headlights shining into piles of old tires, broken furniture and black garbage bags torn to shreds by, Darkly imagined, giant grizzlies. Banana skins, peanut butter jars, and empty baked bean tins were strewn across the site, but no bear was to blame. A gang of hunchbacked raccoons had claimed the spoils.

About fifteen minutes into the family trek, the road began a steady, gentle incline, with the hardwood trees giving way to conifers, until they reached a clearing on a bluff over-looking a valley.

Darkly could make out a narrow river flowing under two bridges in the center of the town of Wolf Woods hundreds of feet below. She recognized a church from its green copper steeple and a main street of red brick buildings surrounded by around thirty worn, white clapboard homes. No people or moving cars were in sight. Strange. A ghost town?

Jack brought the RV up alongside a waist-high decrepit, wooden railing. It was the only thing between them and a sheer drop down to the valley below. They now sat on the highest point overlooking the river and town.

"How's that for a view?" asked Jack. "Much better than a crowded campsite."

Catharine warily eyed the edge of the precipice.

"Do you think we're a little close?"

Jack killed the engine.

"Honey, that railing looks like it's been there a hundred years. Nothing's broken through yet. We're fine."

"You know what I meant."

"Don't worry about it tonight. We're a speck on the mountain." Then he whispered, "I promise they'll hear us out. You're the answer to their prayers."

Jack climbed out of the driver's seat and made his way back to the side door to let in the fresh air.

After an entire day of air conditioning, Darkly also melted willingly into the blast of warm air.

"I want to help."

While Catharine unlatched cupboards, Darkly and Jack began the RV's nightly check-off. Jack opened a compartment on the outside of the RV and removed two wheel blocks and two telescoping, aluminum struts. He then reached back in to flick an electric switch.

"I want to do it," Darkly complained.

She pushed her dad out of the way and held the switch down until a whining, electric motor ground to life. A yellow and green-striped canopy slowly unrolled from its hiding place under the roof.

"Okay, but let go the moment it stops or you'll burn the motor out," Jack said as he pet the top of Darkly's head.

"I'm not a dog, Dad," Darkly protested.

Jack just laughed and picked up the wheel blocks. He jammed one under the front driver's wheel and the other under the back passenger wheel, kicking both with his boots until they wouldn't budge. He jogged back to Darkly, grabbed one of the aluminum struts and twisted it into its full length. He popped it into place under one corner of the now fully-opened canopy.

Darkly let go of the switch and passed the second strut to her dad.

"You can stake them in," he said as he propped up the other corner of the canopy, creating an expanse of shade that would accommodate the whole family.

Darkly grabbed four metal stakes and drove them into the dirt, hopping up and down on them until the struts were firmly pinned to the ground.

Jack shook the struts. They barely shifted.

"Good job."

He opened another compartment on the side of the RV and pulled out three folding deck chairs.

Darkly plopped herself down in the smallest of the three and gazed out across the valley towards the western sky. The sun was beginning to set and illuminated the silver river with streaks of gold and red. The valley stretched about two miles wide and ten miles long. The narrow road they turned from followed the river through the town and rose into the hills at either end.

She scanned the slopes leading down to the river. On the other side of the valley, any trees had long since been cut down to make way for pastures. Cows and sheep shared the same grazing grounds above sleepy Wolf Woods. On Darkly's side of the valley, the tree line reached to within a couple yards of the water.

It was while following this tree line that Darkly got her first look at a bear. About a mile to the west of the town, she saw the animal climb up the riverbank. She could barely make it out, but was instantly mesmerized.

"Dad!" Darkly screeched and hopped to her feet. "A bear!"

"I'll grab the binoculars!"

Jack leapt into the RV, while Darkly continued to watch the animal scramble up the riverbank. It lumbered up to the tree cover and was gone.

Jack jumped out of the RV, not bothering with the two retractable steps, and vainly focused the binoculars on the river.

"You missed him. He went into the woods."

Darkly sighed. It had been a brief encounter, but she'd finally seen one.

"Oh well. I've seen bears before. And other things."

Jack turned the attention of his binoculars onto the town below.

Darkly held a set of threes and almost a full run of hearts. All she needed to lay down was a joker or an eight of clubs. Shanghai Rummy was the family ritual after most meals. It was preferable to bedtime stories, and it was something Darkly had become very good at. Jack and Catharine long ago gave up letting her win. When she beat them at cards, it was on the level.

Darkly picked at her plate of grilled cheese crusts she never fully enjoyed until they had grown cold.

It was Catharine's turn to play, and she picked a card off the deck in the center of the table, then discarded the eight of clubs. It was when Darkly reached for that card, the exact card she had been waiting for, that it happened.

The whole RV shook. It felt like another vehicle had rammed into the front of the camper, causing the whole cabin to shudder.

"What the hell?!" Jack exclaimed.

He bolted up and ran to the driver's seat. Out of instinct, Catharine climbed over Darkly and made quickly for the side door to lock it.

Darkly peered out the window next to the RV's built-in table. The moon was a blood orange crescent that reminded Darkly of a carved jack-o'-lantern's eye. She could see the trees blowing in the wind under the moonlight. She could also make out movement, but no shape. She sunk down into the couch, out of sight from whatever was out there.

"Jack?!" Catharine was in full panic mode.

"Don't jump to conclusions. It's probably a moose. They've been known to try to mate with cars."

Jack was grasping.

"We're a really big car, Jack."

Catharine could find time for sarcasm in any situation.

Darkly had an idea. "If it's a bear, maybe it can smell the food."

She began shoving the grilled cheese crusts into her mouth as quickly as she could.

"Darkly, stop! You'll choke yourself."

Catharine sat down next to Darkly and held her close, while, once again, the whole RV shook with an impact. This time, it was on the side by the door.

"Shit. That's a dent."

Jack shot over to the side window and looked out again.

"It's pushed us up against the railing. I'm gonna start up the engine. That'll scare it off."

"Jack, just drive away."

"How am I supposed to do that with the canopy rolled out, Cat?"

"Don't get mad at me."

"I'm not mad."

Jack pulled the keys from his pocket and fumbled nervously with the ignition key, eventually fitting it into the steering column. He turned the engine over, and the RV came to life. Then Jack turned on the headlights.

"Holy shit!"

Darkly saw all the color drain from her father's face. She saw the green and red lights of the dashboard reflected in the glass above the steering wheel. Jack saw something very different. He looked back at Catharine.

"Hold on. I'm going to get us out of here."

"But you said the canopy -"

"Just hold on!"

Jack put the RV into second gear and pressed his foot hard down on the accelerator. The wheels spun, but there was no movement forward. The wheel block at the front of the RV was still in place.

Then they all heard the piercing howl. It sounded almost human, but deeper, with a menacing, underlying growl.

Jack dropped the gear shift into reverse, and the RV immediately shifted backwards, slamming into a curved section of the guard rail.

"We're free," her father said hopefully.

Darkly could hear the canopy ripping and the struts snapping, as her father brought the RV into drive and gunned the engine. The vehicle jerked forward. They were moving.

Jack swung the large steering wheel wildly around to the left and began making his way down the hill.

"Out of the way!" Jack yelled at the thing outside the RV.

A big thud echoed through the cabin, as Jack hit whatever was blocking their escape. Darkly felt the bumps, as first the front, then the back tires ran over something. Then the RV swerved sharply to the right. They were going too fast; Jack was losing control.

Jack pumped the brakes, but the RV was now skidding off the dirt road. Nothing was going to stop it but the trees they were careening into.

The RV rammed a cluster of birch trees. To the sound of branches scraping the windows and sides of the RV, Darkly was thrown under the table. The RV rolled forward in jolts until the trees finally forced it to stop.

Darkly felt the engine sputter out under the floor where she lay, not wanting to open her eyes. She felt her mother pull her close and envelope her body. Then, she heard her father moan and call out, "Everyone okay?"

"I think so," Catharine replied.

Jack tried to turn over the engine several times. Nothing. He turned off the headlights and didn't say a word for several moments.

Darkly knew what was going on. They were waiting. Waiting for whatever was going to happen next. She could feel the cool weight of her necklace on her skin. Darkly picked up the silver moon pendant and stroked it, as she always did in times of stress. The pock marks on the moon were set with shiny black rock. Where the pendant rested on her upper chest, a faint bluish rash covered the skin and spread out in faint rays like spider veins. The same spindly stain marked her thumb and forefinger.

The pendant was not entirely benign. It was painful to wear, bringing what could only be described as a constant, yet minimal, electric shock to the skin, as though the silver content and her body were repelling one another.

Darkly found the pain bearable now, even reassuring in its constancy. But with her arms strapped to her sides as a toddler, the pendant was excruciating. She would scream herself into exhaustion and eventual sleep, while her mother stroked her hair, crying softly and telling her daughter it would save her from a life of misery in the years to come.

Soon after weaning, Darkly's mother and father would leave her one weekend a month in the care of a family friend, so that they could follow their joint lifelong obsession: geology. From the Mojave Desert to the Badlands and the Great Plains, Catharine and Jack MacIntyre hunted one rock only. Meteorite. And in particular, meteorites with concentrations of an element born in supernovas.

With silver recovered from the heavens, Catharine crafted her necklaces. Darkly spent many hours watching her mother bend heated metal into celestial shapes, manipulating the precious metal through thick gloves and pliers. But never did she see her parents sell a single item or wear one themselves.

Before setting out on this family vacation, Darkly watched her mother put down the soldering iron for the last time. She packed several hundred necklaces into a wooden chest and placed it securely in the RV cupboard next to the propane stove-top fuel and the powdered milk.

It could have been three minutes, or an hour, but the next thing did happen. Another piercing, primal howl was followed by more dead silence.

Jack got out of the driver's seat and rubbed his ribs. He crouched down next to Catharine and Darkly.

"What is it, Daddy?"

"Shhhh." Jack put his hand on Darkly's head. "Just be quiet."

He looked deeply into Catharine's eyes. She knew, without him saying so, that he was going to confront what was outside.

"It's why we came here," he said with wavering confidence.

Jack got up and walked slowly to the door. He unlocked it and looked back at his wife and daughter.

"It's okay. I'll be right back. Lock the door behind me."

He stepped out into the darkness.

Catharine left Darkly's side, walked slowly to the door and held her hand over the lock. She hesitated for a second, and then turned it.

Outside, something was coming closer to Jack. The hairs stood up on the back of his neck. The forest was silent, as though the wind itself stopped blowing in anticipation. The earth held its breath.

Inside, Darkly heard her father call out, "We've come back. We don't want any trouble. I'm sorry we ran. You startled us, you see."

Darkly met her mother's eyes, and Catharine pulled her close once again. Darkly heard her mother's heart race and imagined it slowing until it stopped. Like everyone else, young and old, Darkly lived by hope. Hope that her inability to imagine an end to her own life would somehow inoculate those she cared about against the final outcome.

Yet, in this instance, Darkly had a sixth sense that she would feel alone for the rest of her life. She clung to a woman who was already a million miles away from her.

Jack saw the light in their eyes first. His voice shook as he said, "We've come to make our peace. We found a treatment. For your children. For the babies. They don't have to live like this."

Jack's body and senses tingled to the point of vibration. He felt the slightest temperature change on his skin, and a hundred different smells invaded his nostrils, filling his insides. They were everywhere. He looked back at the RV door, where one of them had slipped in behind him unnoticed. Jack's bladder gave out, and he collapsed to the ground, feeling the cool dirt on his palms. Then, they attacked.

Darkly had never witnessed her father cry out in agony, in helplessness, in despair, but she knew it was him when she heard it.

Darkly also knew it was his body breaking when he was thrown against the outside of the RV.

Catharine wiped a tear off Darkly's cheek as she got her up and removed the seat of the couch to reveal an empty storage space below. She lifted Darkly into the space, as the pounding on the door began.

"Whatever you hear, you aren't to come out of here until I come get you. Cover your ears and don't say a single word. Do you understand, sweetheart? Cover your ears."

Darkly nodded.

Catharine acted swiftly, but without panic, and even offered a gentle smile, as she kissed her daughter for what Darkly sensed would be the last time.

Darkly inhaled to sob.

"No crying. What did I say? You can't make a sound."

Catharine stroked Darkly's hair and helped her curl up into the bottom of the storage space. Catharine then ran her fingertips over Darkly's moon pendant. Darkly observed those same fingers recoil, and her mother pull her hand back, tucking it under her arm, nursing an unseen pain.

"And remember what I've always told you. Wear your own personal moon at all times. Never take it off."

And, then, all was darkness.

The inside of the couch had a strong, cedar smell. Darkly couldn't see her hand before her face. She was shaking so hard, she had to hold herself tightly, so as not to make any noise. She took small, silent breaths and listened as the pounding on the RV door became more violent and frantic.

Then the door was ripped open, and the RV tipped, as something or some things climbed inside.

The pent-up emotion in Catharine's voice released itself. "You know who I am. I'm descended from the first of our kind. You will listen to me. Your children don't have to suffer."

Darkly heard her mother's footsteps run to the front of the RV and all matter of hell break loose. What sounded like wild animals tearing each other to pieces ended with something large crashing down on the couch above her. The impact forced the base of the seat to break and cave in over Darkly's head, stopping just an inch above her face.

Darkly knew she was supposed to cup her ears with her hands, but she was paralyzed. The cracked balsa wood now allowed a shard of light into her hiding place and also gave her a slivered glimpse at what was happening to her mother.

Catharine's face was pressed against the floor by some force Darkly couldn't make out. Her skin was splattered with blood. Catharine's eyes widened as she met her daughter's horrified gaze. Darkly watched clouds of yellow swim into the whites of her mother's eyes, and saw her lips contract to hug teeth now clenched in a snarl.

It was then that fear overcame Darkly's conscious mind. Darkness seeped into her brain like a grown-up's drug. The last thing she heard was Catharine whimper like a child, and call for her own mother, as she was dragged out of the RV and into the night.

CHAPTER ONE

Darkly Stewart caught the scent of the man standing next to her under the streetcar shelter. Well, scent was the wrong word. It was like nosing whisky with your mouth open, letting the vapors run across the taste buds. She was standing next to someone who had recently killed another human being. She could taste it. The metallic make-up of his blood mingled with a forbidden sweetness. It was a sweetness that worked its way into the pores of the cheeks and stung the mouth. Strange, he didn't look the type. He had kind eyes. Maybe a soldier on leave? The cropped hair fit the bill.

Darkly had come a long way from the days of an American orphan found walking along the Trans-Canada highway, dehydrated and incoherent, remembering only three things from the first seven years of her life: her name was Darkly Stewart, she was from Portland, Oregon, and she must never remove the silver moon pendant hanging around her neck.

The middle-aged couple from Toronto who rescued Darkly had tried to have children for many years and interpreted their chance encounter as divine intervention. Who's to say they weren't right? It's true they didn't contact the police. But, in his defense, Royal Canadian Mounted Police Constable, William Schilling, did search for Darkly's past in Portland. He prayed he would not, but entirely expected to find a relation, school record, or the smallest clue to his new ward's existence. To the relief of his wife, Elizabeth, he did not. So, Darkly Stewart was raised Darkly Stewart Schilling.

Yes, her parents had pinned upon her a registry of brighter names. Darkly rejected these, clinging tightly to one of the few connections to a forgotten little girl, and the Schillings stopped pinning.

A family friend referred the Schillings to a discreet and costly psychiatrist who advised against prying at all into Darkly's past. Darkly had forgotten for a reason, and it was best to consign such trauma to another life. "Let sleeping dogs lie," opined the psychiatrist. The Schillings happily complied.

As for the moon necklace, Darkly never mentioned the physical pain it inflicted for fear that it would be forcibly removed. The family doctor could find no direct correlation between the necklace and Darkly's blue spider veins, so a previous physical trauma to the chest was deemed the likely culprit. Use of a fake tanning lotion or make-up was suggested to bring the color of the skin back to a healthier complexion. Through her teenage years, Darkly took to wearing turtlenecks to avoid questions altogether.

Constable William Schilling gave no thought to Darkly's future career, and certainly did not expect her to follow in his footsteps, until one family weekend in the Algonquin wilderness revealed Darkly's gift.

Darkly loved family camping trips, slipping out into the woods alone while her parents slept. For her, it was an experience that bordered on the religious. Every leaf caught in the wind and each drop of rain that hit bark connected to Darkly in a way to which others were oblivious.

The Schilling family sought seclusion on their holidays, much as they did during their day-to-day existence, perhaps reluctant to push their luck that someone would recognize Darkly and take her away.

On this particular trip, though, Darkly and her parents shared a campfire with the young couple from the adjacent site. Her father asked her not to stare at the young man, and his girlfriend playfully told the teen to keep her hands off her property. But Darkly could taste the murders within him, which made looking away all the more conspicuous. An instinct welled up within her to hold her ground and stare the dangerous intruder down.

That taste. There were moments in her life when her mouth acted like a canary in a coal mine. Darkly felt as though she was a bullet shooting through the stranger's veins, and she could taste his lust in her mouth. The metallic shades of iron gave way to a potent spice that lit her tongue on fire.

As she curled up in her sleeping bag in the three-man tent later that night, fiercely gripping her moon pendant, she whispered to her father her fears for the life of the young woman.

The next morning, William discovered a body torn to pieces, and the man was never found. To this day, William chooses to believe it was a bear attack. The marks on the girl's body were not made by a human. Of that, he was certain.

So it was, on that morning in the woods, William learned of his daughter's disturbing ability to tell when another had fresh blood on their hands. Thus, he gently guided her to where she found herself today.

With her parents retired to the small cottage community of Parry Sound, Darkly found herself renting a studio apartment in the Queen West neighborhood of Parkdale. The neighborhood was inhabited by two distinct groups of people. Out-of-work, organic-shake-consuming, wannabe-filmmakers dominated the main thoroughfares, wearing army fatigues and riding vintage bicycles built for an age of hoop skirts.

The narrow neighborhood streets, on the other hand, belonged to the diminutive, blue-rinse, Portuguese ladies in sensible shoes, who didn't speak a lick of English and never would. It was a true collision of old and new worlds.

Darkly could have claimed it as part of her cover, but she also genuinely felt at home in places she appeared out-of-place. Her first rule as an undercover Mountie was to always leave herself open to attention. That way, no one would accuse her of hiding anything.

Darkly was attached to missing persons. At twenty-five, she looked nineteen, which her government-issued fake ID attested to. Darkly could be considered perfect in just about every way. There were also some distinct imperfections she kept concealed. Nevertheless, she had a body and a face to which a plastic surgeon would do time for touching.

There was also that jet black hair. It was dramatic when draped across her pale skin, though not off-putting, and, surprisingly, only a couple of young men had been given the opportunity to run their fingers through it. Relationships were very much discouraged during an undercover assignment that could stretch on into years.

She underplayed her looks on her own time: little make-up, her hair tucked under baggy clothing. But, for this assignment, Darkly was instructed to play it up for all she was worth. She boarded the streetcar in tight black leggings and a lace top that stuck to her perspiring skin in the humidity, barely concealing her undergarments.

Disembarking at Queen's Quay, Darkly made her way along the lakeshore to the warehouse complex known as The Senate, an event and clubbing space she would never have been caught dead in as a patron. As the RCMP Constable, her cover was that of a bartender.

At the start of her shift, Darkly cleaned her bar surface, counted-in the till, cut her garnishes, and restocked the beer. Not that she would serve much beer. The Senate, *the* downtown club destination for anyone under thirty, was not known for its alcohol consumption.

Darkly entered the club down a long red carpet past the bouncers stationed between fake Roman columns. The main foyer had a tacky, naked goddess pouring water from a jug into a pool of water below, known as the bottomless wishing well. Legend had it that the more change a guy threw into the well, the better his chances of getting lucky that night. The club's owner, Dmitri, fostered this legend for obvious reasons.

The problem was that the guys didn't want the girls seeing them throw the coins into the fountain. Dmitri, being the clever Greek he was, placed the women's toilets inside the club, and the men's in the foyer. The coat check girls were never short of entertainment, though they were also the ones who had to dredge out the collection well each night, which supposedly went to Dmitri's son's college fund. Dmitri's wife had met her husband while working as one of his coat check girls.

Leaving the foyer, the guest had a choice of entering two large rooms. One was known as The Orgy. The floor was covered in wide, backless couches overflowing with plush, multicolored cushions. The walls were painted with Roman aristocrats depicted indulging in numerous sins.

The other room was the Temple of Venus. Fake torches lined the textured foam stone walls, and in the center of the room, there was the large statue of the immodest Goddess Venus emerging from an oyster shell. Small granite-top stools were dotted around the room for the ladies to sit on while the men did what they were there to do: buy the drinks and harass Darkly's alter ego.

Once six o'clock rolled around, Juan wheeled in the dolly full of water bottles. There were three bartenders in the Temple: Darkly, Chad, and Samantha, Darkly's blonde double.

Juan dropped eight cases of water at each one of the bars. Darkly pulled out two-hundred and twenty bucks from her pocket and handed it to the cheery Mexican. She always gave him twenty bucks extra. He was the only genuine person who stepped foot in the place. He reminded her that none of this was real. She even envied him. He was happy just to live in a safe city and enjoy a little job security.

The Senate was not a pub. People did not come here to drink and chat. They came here to dance and to pick out a partner for the night. The first thing they did before getting out of their cars, was inhale or swallow something illegal. The girls would order one cosmo, the fellas, a crown and coke, and then it was water for the rest of the night.

That's not why Darkly was here. Her superiors couldn't care less about youthful excess and ecstasy. What did keep them up at night was the disappearance of five women in under a year, all of whom were last seen at The Senate. Darkly was assigned to determine if The Senate was the headquarters of a trafficking ring, and if so, to shut it down.

The deal with the water was simple. The bartenders paid for their own bottles, then charged whatever they wanted to the customers. Dmitri took home half the take, the rest went to the staff. This was the busiest night of the week, and the 905'ers, those souls unfortunate enough to live in the area code beyond sight of the phallic CN Tower, would be out in droves and eager to impress their dates.

"Five a bottle?" Chad yelled out.

Darkly and Samantha gave Chad the thumbs up. They could get that much on a Friday night. With sales and tips, Darkly should clear as much as $800. That was most of her rent. And the RCMP let her keep it. She referred to it as her hazard pay.

Among the 905'ers, were the Italian men in their tailored black slacks and white shirts, as well as too much expensive cologne.

Their girlfriends wore black with red accents, and always two sizes too small for their body type. Together, the couples looked like they were all attending the same convention. None of them ever seemed to notice this fact.

The Russians, still stigmatized by the label of communism, had to wear the most noticeably-branded Western clothing they could find. Everything --from their running shoes, to their jeans, to their t-shirts and sunglasses-- displayed large shiny initials, and you could bet they weren't knock-offs. The combination of so many separate items of ostentatious clothing reminded Darkly of old SNL sketches about "wild and crazy guys."

Finally, there were the Asians. They wore the latest in hip-hop casual wear, with emphasis on the shoes, ball caps, and gold chains. They traveled in large groups that Darkly and the other bartenders referred to as "triads."

Thanks to these cooks, dishwashers, secretaries, insurance brokers, make-up counter girls, waiters, and nurses, a bartender only had to work two to three nights a week to make a decent living.

It was just as the doors opened at 8pm on a Friday night, and the first group of date-less girls walked into the Temple, hours before any man they'd crave would show up, that Darkly received the text from her partner.

Lawrence was Filipino and worked The Senate crowd from the other side of the bar.

Darkly looked down at her beeping phone and opened her inbox. *I'm in.*

Lawrence was in his early thirties, but looked in his twenties. With years more undercover experience, he called the shots on this operation. He was responsible for Darkly's well-being.

Weeks before Darkly found her way onto the club staff, Lawrence was spending a night a week at The Senate. He chatted up other clubbers until a group accepted him as one of their extended family. To the bouncers and staff, he was indistinguishable from the other triad members. He'd have been pretty crappy at his job if he wasn't. But, Darkly had been an employee now for over a month, and still they were no closer to presenting a warrant.

At three in the morning, after she'd closed down her section of the bar, she would walk alone along the quay, presenting herself as easy prey, confident in her own self-defense training, Lawrence's close proximity, and the lipstick-size canister of bear spray Darkly kept strapped to her thigh. No one had considered her appetizing yet.

It was ten at night, during the busiest point of the evening, when the girl walked in. Teased blond hair, pretty, but a face aged by years of contempt, and the kind of lips that were either set in a scowl or the occasional forced smile. Her clothes were outdated and a mishmash of several decades: her leather pants were out of the eighties, her ripped t-shirt from the 90's, and the scarf around her neck looked like a prop from a 1970's production of *Grease*.

"You are a mess, girl," Darkly said under her breath.

Marielle scanned the crowd. She spotted a group of young men huddled in a corner. They were the typical university freshmen who hadn't yet outgrown their awkward high school years. Marielle walked right up to the shortest of the three and smiled.

"Buy me a drink?" she asked rather forcefully.

"Sure."

Shorty separated himself from his herd. His stutter exposed his lack of confidence.

"I'm- I'm Tom."

"Marielle."

They made their way to the bar, as they were supposed to.

Tom looked downright virginal and out of his depth. Darkly had seen it before and knew exactly how this would go down. Marielle's boyfriend probably cheated on her, and now she's come out hunting for revenge sex. Tom will fall madly in-love, but in the morning, it will feel like a huge mistake for Marielle. Oh well, it was the kind of education Tom went to university to receive.

"What do you like to drink?" Tom asked, pulling out his wallet.

"Whatever you're having," Marielle replied.

Tom ordered two Bud Lights from Darkly and disappeared into a corner with Marielle.

The rest of the night went smoothly despite a couple of the usual incidents where someone got too high and threw up on the floor. But, as the crowd thinned out, Lawrence winked at Darkly and left The Senate to take up his position outside by the quay. An hour from now, he'd keep pace with a streetcar that wound its way alongside the curve of the lakefront until reaching Darkly's home.

Darkly counted her money, handed Dmitri's cut to one of the bouncers, and made her way to the toilets. It had been a hot night, one of the hottest of the summer. Darkly wet some paper towels and patted herself down with cold water, wiping away the make-up that covered the blue spider veins in that shallow valley between her breasts.

It was then she heard the heavy breathing behind her. The breathing quickly evolved into the sound of a man moaning and climaxing. Darkly banged on the toilet stall.

"Do it in your car, for Christ's sake. It's time to go home."

"Sorry."

She recognized the voice that was accompanied by the banging around that getting dressed involves in tight quarters. Tom unlocked the stall and rushed past Darkly and out the women's room.

Marielle and Darkly faced off.

Darkly was about to tell the other girl to grow some self-respect, but was stopped dead in her tracks by a sight she never would have imagined she'd see on any body but her own. Marielle's scarf lay on the ground in front of the toilet. She pulled her t-shirt down over her breasts, and pulled her hair free. There on her body was the same pattern of blue spider veins that Darkly had been marked with so long ago. There was no pendant.

Marielle also recognized the same veins on Darkly. Her eyes expressed confusion for a moment, analyzing from a distance the necklace Darkly wore. Then her eyes turned blatantly hostile.

Darkly broke the silence with, "Who are you?"

Marielle responded with a hard punch to Darkly's gut, taking her by surprise and knocking her backwards into the sink, completely winded.

As Marielle raced out the door of the toilets, Darkly caught her breath and chastised herself for letting her guard down. In pursuit, she hightailed it out of the toilets and through the club entrance into the parking lot. The last of the clubbers were piling into designated drivers' vehicles. Tom and Marielle were nowhere to be seen.

Darkly pulled out her phone to text Lawrence.

Something's happened. Heading your way.

She didn't send it. How was she supposed to explain what happened? What would it even mean to say she'd been punched in the gut by a girl with the same identical birthmark as her? This was a missing persons' investigation, not an episode of *The X-Files*.

Lawrence had first met Darkly during her training. The recruits were required to take on an experienced officer in hand-to-hand combat. Most of the male officers went easy on the female recruits. Not Lawrence. Darkly was sore for a week, and she thanked Lawrence for it. He followed her career from that point on and recruited her to his division at the first opportunity.

Darkly put her phone away and began making her way to the quay.

An old ferry permanently docked at the quay had been converted into a fish restaurant. The fact it could no longer move under its own engines earned it a place on the tourist maps. The RCMP had alerted the owner to this operation and had a key to the eyesore. This late at night, all the staff were long home, but Lawrence, his car stashed behind a nearby liquor store, stood in the wheel house, binoculars glued to his face, watching Darkly's every step.

Darkly first spotted the van out of the corner of her eye. It was a white, nondescript delivery van, with no company markings. The driver drove at a steady pace and quickly passed Darkly. At the next traffic light, she watched the van make a U-turn and drive back towards her. Talk about bad timing.

She was under two hundred yards from the ferry, when she saw the wheel house door swing open and Lawrence make his way down the gangplank to the dock. The van picked up speed and skidded to a stop, blocking Darkly from her route to the quay.

The man who jumped out of the passenger side was big. A lot bigger than Darkly. But she had used that size difference to her benefit before. Once she got him on his back, getting up wouldn't be so easy.

He was on her fast. Surprisingly, his size didn't inhibit his speed. Darkly lifted the bear spray in the palm of her hand to firing position, and the lug knocked it flying. Darkly ducked the grab that followed and slid her foot under her assailant's left leg. He was immovable, like a mountain. Darkly steadied herself into a defensive position. The man smiled through a bushy goatee beard and lunged. She successfully dodged and retaliated with a slam of the palm of her hand into the man's nose. He grunted, but didn't move.

Suddenly, he charged like a linebacker. As Darkly side-stepped, he countered, forcing her to back up into the arms of what she could only guess was the driver. When those arms lifted her off the ground and tossed her to the side, Darkly saw it was Marielle.

Were they a team? She looked at the van, where the driver's confused reflection in the side mirror matched his partner's. Darkly guessed not. Marielle was clearly a stranger to them both.

She crouched down and circled the big man, as he chuckled. Was she trying to save Darkly? She felt like the trophy at a prize fight.

With the agility of an animal, Marielle now charged her challenger, grabbed hold of his right hand, and used it to pull herself quickly onto his back. She slammed both of her open palms against the man's ears, and he screamed out in pain. She then bit into one of his ears. He collapsed to his knees.

The driver leapt out of the van, and at that moment, Marielle pulled a knife from her back and speedily slit the mountain of a man's lifeline. She turned to the driver, blood dripping from her mouth and knife. He scampered back into the idling van, locked the door, and put it into drive.

As the van sped off, Darkly got to her feet and approached the man she had been waiting to capture for months. She wasn't sure how much use he would be to her dead. His last breaths were a gurgle of air and blood. What the hell just happened?

Lawrence was still fifty yards away, when Marielle lowered her head and caught Darkly's stare in her own. She approached Darkly slowly. The blood dripped down Marielle's chin and found its way into her cleavage, racing the blue lines of the spider veins. A few inches from Darkly, she stopped, bizarrely sniffing the air in front of Darkly. Her gaze then fell to Darkly's pendant.

With hesitant fingers, she reached out to within a couple millimetres of the silver necklace. She brushed it with her fingertips. It was like a jolt from an electric socket.

Marielle leapt back, and hugged her hand. She sucked on her fingers, as if soothing a burn. Seconds later, she leveled her gaze on Darkly again and whispered, "Heretic." She then raised her knife into the air, ready to stab down into Darkly's breast, and screamed.

Darkly had not tasted death on this one earlier in the night, but she knew that was her intent. A shot rang out, and Marielle was thrown back onto the ground, dead.

Darkly looked behind her. Lawrence stood twenty yards away, his gun raised in the kill position. It was over. Or so Darkly thought.

The driver of the van had not been far away. She heard him gun the engine and watched helpless as he barreled down on her and Lawrence. Of course, he was coming back for the other man's body. The body would lead them right to him.

Lawrence caught up with Darkly, and they both now ran for their lives, with the van gaining ground behind them.

"Keep running," Lawrence yelled at Darkly. "That's an order."

Lawrence stopped, turned, and began firing into the cab's windshield, as Darkly veered off to the right, racing back to the relative safety of The Senate. Seconds before the van was on him, one of Lawrence's bullets found its target. Blood rained down inside the van, as the front grill struck Darkly's partner full on. Running over Lawrence's broken body, the lifeless driver of the van collapsed onto the wheel, involuntarily turning the vehicle towards the quay.

Darkly stopped running, and looked back. To her horror, Lawrence was in the fetal position on the ground, not moving. She ran faster than she ever had in her life. She kneeled and turned Lawrence onto his back. He was still gripping his gun.

She gently lifted his head into her arms and looked into his eyes.

"You're not alone," she told him.

She repeated this phrase over and over, until she saw the light in his eyes go dull. She pulled Lawrence into her, holding him as tightly as she could, then looked up at the moon hovering above them both. The tears she wept for Lawrence had been pent up inside her for a lifetime.

CHAPTER TWO

It was routine procedure. Darkly was required to be examined by a physician, and it was a good thing, too. Despite thinking she had come through last night's bloodbath scathed only in the mind, she had, in fact, suffered a couple of bruised ribs. A little rest, some painkillers, and no heavy lifting were what the doctor prescribed.

That was nothing compared to what was coming. She'd be debriefed, and then ordered to take a holiday with pay. Your partner's dead, and you're told to go on vacation, for Christ's sake, where you can brood for hours over what you could have done differently. The system didn't make any sense.

Darkly sat on the hospital bed, while her mother sat in a chair to her left, occasionally reaching out for Darkly's hand, squeezing it and smiling without saying anything. Her dad sat at the end of the bed, watching the television.

The news showed the white van that ran Lawrence down being pulled out of Lake Ontario. Water poured out of the windows, and the cameraman gave his audience just a glimpse of a face resting against the steering wheel, before a plain-clothes officer walked into shot and blocked the view.

"Jesus wept, William. Turn it off."

Darkly's father did as his wife said, but gave his daughter a knowing look. He knew she would have preferred it left on.

"You'll be told to take some time off."

"I know."

Her mother reached over and squeezed Darkly's hand again. "Oh, you could come visit your father and me. Wouldn't you like that, darling?"

"Maybe she wants to be alone, Elizabeth."

"There's a guest room. She can close the door if she wants to be alone."

This got Elizabeth out of her chair, hovering over her daughter.

"If the door's shut, I know not to bother you. I just think you should have someone to talk to. Close by." Before he could reply for Darkly, Elizabeth cut her husband off. "That's all I'm going to say about it."

"I'll think about it." Darkly tried to sound enthusiastic for her mother's sake.

At that moment, the man who Darkly and Lawrence received their orders from, Sergeant Vincetti, knocked and entered the room. He wore his dress red uniform and carried his Stetson hat. His longer than regulation hair indicated a general distrust of the rules born out of many years of undercover duties well before Darkly's time.

"Constable. Mr. and Mrs. Schilling."

Darkly's parents stood up, and Darkly herself made to get out of bed. This was the first moment she noticed the pain, and her hand shot to her side.

"Please don't get up. That's an order," Vincetti said.

"Yes sir."

"Did you catch any more of the bastards? Or are they all dead?" William asked.

Darkly gave her sergeant a look of empathy for the drilling he was about to receive from her father.

"What's the next step?"

"You served in the arctic, didn't you, sir? Brought in that serial killer in 1979? The one feeding Inuit children to his dogs?"

Elizabeth winced. Vincetti was going to butter her husband up with gruesome recollections.

"I'm very sorry, Mrs. Schilling. You wear bluntness like a tie in my line of work."

William glossed over the younger man's lack of tact.

"That was me, sergeant, and without the satellites or mobile phone records to guide me. Not like today. Just witness accounts and tracks in the snow."

William drifted off deeper into the past.

"When he finally realized he couldn't shake me, he took off all his clothes and went to sleep in the snow. Figured he'd let the cold take him before he faced a court of law. He was still alive when I found him. I put the cuffs on him, then dragged him into a bed roll with me. I was butt naked, and I damn well raised his body temperature."

"William, he doesn't want to hear all about that."

"On the contrary, Mrs. Schilling, I do. But, another time. Over a pint maybe."

William shut up, nodded his head, and Vincetti turned his full attention to Darkly.

"We ran the prints on both men. Both had criminal records as long as Christmas. That led us to several addresses. At a suburban home, at six-thirty this morning, we found one of the missing girls."

Darkly held her breath.

"Alive," Vincetti continued after the suspenseful pause. "We'll find the rest."

Darkly breathed again.

Sergeant Vincetti put on his Stetson to leave.

"Please report to my office at nine in the morning for debriefing, Constable. I'll require a written report, as well."

"Yes, sir. What did you find out about the woman?"

"Nothing. No ID. Her prints and DNA led us nowhere. It's like she doesn't exist. But, we'll keep looking. I'm sorry about Lawrence. He was a good officer. A good man. I'm going to pay my respects to his family now."

"I'd like to be there, sir."

Darkly stood up, as Vincetti opened the door to the room.

"That's not a good idea. Not yet."

Vincetti gave Darkly a half smile and closed the door behind him.

Darkly rode in silence in the back seat of her parents' car on the way back to her apartment. They tried to convince her to stay with them at a downtown hotel. But, it wouldn't have done her any good. So, she agreed to meet them for breakfast at seven-thirty, when she hoped she could convince them to drive back home and stop worrying about her.

Then again, maybe time with her parents was just what she needed. She had felt herself becoming distant, as she dived deeper into her cover. It was like her real life had become the fantasy, and her cover reality.

Elizabeth gave Darkly a big hug, kissed her daughter, and then wiped lipstick off her cheek.

"I'm your mother. You know I won't stop worrying about you, and I'll always be here. I'm just a phone call away."

"I know, mum."

"Okay then."

Elizabeth teared up a little and got back in the car. William saluted his daughter from behind the wheel.

"Constable."

Darkly saluted him back. She unlocked her front door and collapsed onto the futon bed moments after walking inside. She didn't wake up until ten that night.

Darkly reached out of the shower for her cup of coffee and took a sip. Drops from the shower head watered down the coffee. She took a final sip and dumped the rest down the drain. She then got out, dried off and dressed in a navy blue sweat suit, tucking her damp hair under the hood. She still had to write her report, but how could she write a full report if half of it didn't make sense?

Who was that woman? Why the hell did she have the same condition as Darkly? And if Marielle had a silver allergy too, why did she call Darkly a heretic? In that case, wouldn't Marielle be a heretic, as well? What was the heresy they had both committed? And the most important question of all, why did she try to kill Darkly? Darkly had to start finding answers now. Unfortunately, she was about to be handed a series of more peculiar questions.

Darkly grabbed a slice of pizza at the place on the corner, then hopped on the streetcar back down to the hospital. She was willing to bet the body hadn't been moved to the RCMP's forensics lab yet. She needed a little more girl time with Marielle, and this time she was bringing her gun.

Darkly had been leaning against the wall for two hours when she finally caught a break. A couple of times, a nurse had opened the back door to the loading dock and stood in the doorway for a smoke. This despite the No Smoking sign.

Each time, when the cigarette was finished, he slammed the door shut behind him. But, this time, a janitor opened the door to let in a Cintas delivery man. He carried a pile of pink surgical smocks wrapped tightly in cellophane. The janitor propped the door open and left the delivery man to it.

Darkly timed the delivery man three times. Each visit inside took two minutes and change. The fourth time, Darkly walked quickly from the dumpster to the loading dock. She jumped into the back of the Cintas truck and grabbed a box labeled talcum powder. Once out of the truck, she looked around the corner of the door frame. The coast was clear.

She slipped inside the hospital and made her way down a hallway off the boiler room and incinerator. At a T-junction, she could see the delivery man emerging from a supply room empty-handed. She made a left and walked with a sense of purpose.

She decided to hum. People who hum are where they are supposed to be, right? So, while humming *Fly Me To The Moon*, Darkly found herself at another junction, where a sign on the wall pointed to Admittance, Emergency Room, and Morgue.

After another right and a left, she found herself standing in front of two swinging doors. Behind her, she heard someone else whistling the same tune she'd just stopped humming. It was contagious. She pushed her way into the dark room and waited until the whistling grew quiet.

To her left was the medical examiner's office and lab. Beyond that, were four empty examination tables with drains that led to pipes that emptied into grates in the floor. Beyond the tables, were storage coolers that could accommodate twenty-four bodies.

Darkly put the box down on one of the tables and pulled a penlight from her back pocket. She shone the light on the name plates on the refrigerator doors. She scanned several, until finding Lawrence Aragon. She touched the piece of paper that said his name. Should she pray?

There really was no time for sentimentality. She kept walking past several other names, among which she assumed were the occupants of last night's white van. She reached a plate that read "Jane

Doe." This had to be it. Though Darkly had informed Vincetti of Marielle's name, without any documentation to back that up, it was assumed to be an alias. Darkly had convinced Vincetti there was no point in searching for Marielle's one-night stand from the toilet. At least, it shouldn't be a priority. She was convinced he was absolutely innocent.

Darkly opened the door to the refrigerated body storage unit and pulled out the shelf that held a body bag matching Marielle's size. She put the penlight in her mouth and unzipped the bag, revealing Marielle's face. The girl looked as though she could just be sleeping. Her cheeks even looked ruddy. Darkly unzipped the entire bag. Marielle was still dressed, and her clothing was stained with her own blood.

Darkly waved the light over the upper chest. The blue of the spider veins was as vibrant in death as it had been in life. She brushed her fingertips over the veins and moved down Marielle's shirt to the dried blood over her abdomen. She lifted the t-shirt up to reveal the bullet wound. Remarkably, the hole was tiny, as though it had almost healed. The skin around the wound had a purplish bruising.

Darkly let the shirt fall and reached for one of Marielle's hands. She knew the fingernails continued to grow after death, but this was ridiculous. The nails were a couple inches in length, and the back of her hand was covered in a light down of prickly hairs. Darkly looked down at her own nails and the shaved back of her hand.

As a child, she would bite her nails down to the quick, tearing them out of the skin, leaving painful and bloody corners that would be filled with new growth hours later. She filed them once in the morning and once at night in order to keep them at a manageable length. And she could forget nail polish. That would only bring attention to the bizarre condition.

Darkly unlaced one of Marielle's shoes, which were name brand knock-offs she had probably picked up for a few bucks. Darkly pulled off the dirty sock and found the same condition on Marielle's foot.

"Well, you had no problem getting a date last night. I guess there's hope for me."

Darkly zipped the bag back up and slid the tray back into storage. The door clicked shut. As she took two steps away, towards the swinging doors, an almighty clang rang out. Darkly just about jumped out of her skin. She turned to look behind her. Again, another clang, and the door to Marielle's unit shook. Marielle was alive and kicking the door? Impossible!

With the next clang, the handle to the door strained against its latch, stretching the metal. Darkly's eyes went to the box of talcum, and her father's words about footprints in the snow leapt to mind. She tore the box open and emptied a container of powder onto the floor.

Seconds later, Darkly was in the medical examiner's office, with the door shut, and hiding under the desk. Another massive bang, and she heard the handle to the refrigerator unit door catapult across the room, hit the glass of the office wall, and land on the floor. Marielle was out.

"Shit," Darkly whispered to herself, then covered her own mouth.

Above her head, there was a small table lamp. The on-off was a pedal switch, and she'd just turned it on by accidentally sitting on it. She quickly turned it off, just as she heard Marielle's body slump to the floor.

There was absolute quiet for a few moments, but then a click-clack on the floor as Marielle walked towards the office. It sounded like nails on tile floor. Of course! She hadn't put Marielle's shoe back on. The girl's long nails were scraping against the floor.

Darkly sank deeper under the desk, as Marielle walked up to the office door and stopped. Darkly quietly removed the standard-issue revolver from her shoulder holster and glued her eyes to the doorknob on the office door. Surely, Marielle was going to open it. But, then, the click-clacking resumed, and Darkly heard the doors to the morgue swing open. Once again, all was quiet.

It must have been ten minutes before Darkly could work up the nerve to crawl out from under the desk and open the door.

Back in the morgue, she shone her penlight on Marielle's refrigerator unit. Empty, except for Marielle's clothes ripped to pieces. On the floor, where she expected to find footprints, she observed not human prints in the powder, but large animal paw prints. These paw prints guided Darkly to the door and out into the hallway.

With her gun held at the ready, Darkly burst through the swinging doors. No Marielle in sight, but the white powder prints were easy to follow.

As she turned the last corner back to the loading dock, Darkly heard a man scream out in terror and pain. She ran the rest of the way to the loading dock, slammed up against the door frame, and took the safety off her revolver. She counted to three and bolted through the open door.

She found the delivery man rolling in agony. He gripped the side of his torso, which looked like a shark had bitten him. A chunk was missing, and he was bleeding profusely. Darkly holstered her gun and bent down to apply pressure to the man's wound.

She caught movement in the corner of her eye, looked up, and saw the hindquarters of an animal disappear over a concrete wall behind the dumpster.

Darkly turned her attention back to the delivery man.

"What did you see? What was it?"

He just shook his head and passed out from the pain. Once more, all Darkly could do now was yell for help.

CHAPTER THREE

Sergeant Vincetti never blinked. It was the strangest thing. Darkly once entertained the thought her superior had inner transparent eyelids, like an amphibian, that made his outer ones merely cosmetic. Or did he practice for hours in the mirror in order to intimidate young constables with his authority?

"Tell me again. What were you hoping to find at the morgue?"

"I told you, I don't know. You can ask me as many times as you like."

"I will ask you as many times as it takes to get an answer I'm satisfied with, Constable. Why did you feel the need to examine the body of Jane Doe?"

Vincetti liked Darkly, and he had great respect for her father, but he was losing his patience. In a couple of hours, he would need to explain to his superiors what the hell happened last night. And so far, Darkly was only muddying the waters.

"I had a hunch that—"

"That?"

Here it was. The moment of truth.

"You've always told me to follow my gut. Well, I had a hunch that Jane Doe and I are related."

"You mean you've seen her before? Family reunions, photographs?"

"No. We have the same birthmark."

"And what do you think that means?"

"She wasn't connected to the undercover investigation. And I could see in her eyes, when she was holding the knife, that killing me was something she felt she had to do. Should do."

Vincetti just sat there for a moment in silence, not knowing what to make of any of it.

Finally, he answered, "Okay, what's next?"

"I'll find her."

"Do you know where to look?"

Vincetti was fishing, even though he knew the fish would be too small.

"I have a hunch."

"Another hunch. You are officially on paid leave for thirty days, Constable."

Vincetti actually blinked. Darkly understood. She was on her own, without support.

"What are you going to say in your report, sir?"

"A man was attacked by a wild dog. You saved him from bleeding to death."

Darkly did not tell the tale quite as it had happened. In the official version, Marielle had walked out, as a wild, rabid dog had walked in. With the choice between saving a life and chasing a criminal, Darkly chose the life.

"And what about Jane Doe, sir?"

"God knows how many drugs that girl had racing through her veins. People have been mistaken for being dead before. You're dismissed, Constable."

Darkly tried to relax. She and her mother went for walks during the day, and she watched cop shows on the TV at night with her father.

It was a guilty pleasure to identify the massive holes in procedural dramas with William. Each opening scene seemed to involve a plain-clothes detective whispering, squinting, and drinking a cup of coffee, while examining some corpse's mouth for parasites.

But, three nights into her enforced sabbatical, Darkly was finding it harder and harder to scratch her itch with quality family time.

After seeing an image of Darkly on the television in full-dress uniform at Lawrence's funeral, William finally grabbed hold of the tusks of the elephant in the room.

"You blame yourself for your partner's death."

"Dad, I don't want–"

"You should."

"What?"

Was he using reverse psychology on her? She didn't appreciate the tough love. What was wrong with just sitting in front of the TV and pretending everything was normal?

"You weren't carrying a firearm."

"I was ordered not to. If it had been discovered while I was undercover–"

"With a firearm, you could have apprehended the suspects before the situation escalated. Shot out the tires of the van before it had the opportunity to run down your partner."

"Dad, I was ordered not to carry a firearm."

Did he not know what Darkly had been through? She held her partner dead in her arms. She was the last person to hear him breathe instead of a son or daughter at the end of a very long life.

"A good officer knows what orders to disobey."

William turned the TV off and got out of his recliner.

"I'm going to bed."

"We may have lost control of the situation, but there were unexpected variables."

She was sounding guilty to herself now.

"You were never in control of the situation, Darkly."

That was the nail in the coffin, and Darkly could no longer bring herself to respond.

William softened. "You made a mistake. Own it. You'll sleep better."

Neither father nor daughter had anything further to say that night.

The next morning, William made himself scarce, and Darkly sat staring at a breakfast she couldn't stomach. Her mother ate everything on her plate. She always did, even when she was sick. The secret to good health, Elizabeth loved to say, was to stick to a proven pattern and not to deviate. It's the multiple shocks of a thousand deviations building up inside you that kills.

Darkly knew this was ridiculous and that her mother had quite a number of truisms at the ready to explain away her fear of change. But, this morning, Elizabeth Schilling deviated. She ventured into her daughter and husband's private world, a world she wasn't supposed to understand.

After carrying her empty plate and Darkly's undisturbed one to the kitchen, she disappeared into the bedroom for a minute and returned with a yellowed scrapbook.

"Before your father gets back from the lodge, I want to show you something."

Elizabeth flipped through pages of black and white news clippings and stopped on the page displaying a photograph of a man in his late twenties, head bowed, being led away from a residential home in handcuffs.

"Your father considers this man his greatest mistake."

Darkly pulled the book closer.

"Who is he?"

"His name is Ed Laving. It happened two years before you came to us. You brought your father back from the desperate place he lived in thanks to this man. God knows I couldn't reach him."

Darkly had never heard her mother speak like this before. She scanned the article.

"He killed his wife, his children?"

She looked more closely at the photograph. In the home's doorway, Darkly could make out a younger version of her father holding a handkerchief to his mouth. This man wasn't the rock who had raised her.

"Your father first noticed Mrs. Laving at the supermarket. He bumped into her, and she reacted as though she was cut with a knife. He thought it was strange she wore long sleeves in hot weather and never took off her sunglasses. He took an interest. When the scarf around her neck slipped to reveal two burn marks, the kind made with a cigarette, your father decided he would keep an eye on the family. On Mr. Laving in particular."

Darkly felt the newspaper clipping between her fingers, while her eyes remained glued to her mother's. She was enthralled not just by what her mother was saying, but by what her mother was projecting. Elizabeth had lost William years before to his work, to the victims' plight, to the love of the law he shared with Darkly. Elizabeth was cut out; she was a necessity, not a passion. But, lately, since giving up the law, William had begun a journey back to his wife.

"A few nights staking out the house, and your father heard Mrs. Laving's screams. And the children."

"What did he do?"

"He forced his way into the house, handcuffed Ed Laving, and demanded to examine the children."

"And?"

"There wasn't a scratch on them. Ed Laving punished his children indirectly. Dirt under their fingernails, and Ed slapped his wife. Not finishing their supper, and it might be a punch to her stomach. A poor grade ended up as a cigarette burn on her neck."

"I don't understand." Darkly pointed to the newspaper article. "It says they all died."

"Ed Laving was the son of a city councillor who was a close personal friend of your father's sergeant. Mr. Laving was released after only one night of jail, and your father was told not to harass the family anymore."

Elizabeth closed the book.

"Your father could have gone over the head of his sergeant, but he followed orders. Mrs. Laving and her children were dead three days later."

Elizabeth got up from the table.

"I'm going to make a cup of tea. Do you want one?"

"No. Thank you."

"Ed Laving is up for parole for the first time this week, so your father's a bit on edge. Don't take it so personally."

Elizabeth left her daughter to dwell on the demons that haunted her father.

Over Sunday roast that evening, William offered an olive branch. As he passed Darkly the Yorkshire puddings, he told her truthfully, "It's been nice to have you home."

Elizabeth smiled. The ice was broken.

"It's been good to be home, Dad."

"Your mother thinks there's something you haven't told us. About that night."

Darkly frowned in her mother's general direction.

"Your mother is very intuitive," William elaborated.

William reached out and gave Elizabeth's hand a squeeze.

"When I broke that embezzlement case, it was your mother who told me it had to be a woman."

Elizabeth answered Darkly's look. "If it had been a man, there would have been a trail of obvious spending. It was hidden in her children's trust funds."

William continued the story. "She may have been a criminal, but she was providing for her family."

"While her husband was spending the honest money on a mid-life crisis," Darkly's mother finished.

Her mother rarely allowed herself such a moment of smugness.

"You were always an introspective girl, closed off—"

"Mum—"

Elizabeth continued, "Closed off, sometimes, to the help that only those who love you most can give."

"I lost my partner."

"It's more than that. Look at your hand."

Darkly's eyes darted to both of her hands. Her right hand was covered in a web of blue veins.

Her mother sighed. "I still check on you in the middle of the night. I can't help myself. Whenever you wrapped your hands around that necklace in your sleep, there was nothing I could do to pry them free."

Darkly gave in to the cross-examination.

"The woman in the hospital, the dead woman, she had the same markings as me."

William turned his attention to his plate of food and brushed Darkly's concern aside. "Many people have allergies."

"Not like this." Darkly held up her hand.

William opened the road atlas to a page of great open spaces and only a few red lines, representing country roads. There was a long, straight yellow line representing the Trans-Canada highway. William placed his fingertip on a section of the highway.

"This is where we picked you up."

Darkly pointed to a blue dot adjacent to the yellow line.

"What's that dot?"

"A town."

"It doesn't have a name."

Darkly flipped to the map key at the beginning of the book.

"It says here that it's an abandoned settlement."

"Many towns sprang up overnight during the gold rush. They were left behind by the early twentieth century for more prosperous settlements along the railway lines."

"What if people still lived there?"

William removed his reading glasses and grasped the edge of the map page. With one quick flick of the wrist, he ripped the page from the book and handed it to Darkly.

"What if?" her dad asked.

CHAPTER FOUR

"Some coffee with your cream?"

The thirty-something, unshaven young man smiled at Darkly as he opened a pack of sugar and dumped it into his own Starbucks grande coffee. The airport terminal was packed with morning business travelers.

Darkly gave him the hint of a smile. Just the corner of her mouth. She would be polite, but didn't want to encourage him. She continued to pour the cream into her own coffee until it threatened to spill over the rim.

"Better take a sip."

She ignored him and dumped some of the liquid into the stainless steel garbage hole. Starbucks employees—or "partners" as they preferred to be called—must hate people like her.

"I'm flying to Van this morning. You?"

He clearly thought he had a shot. He was sure to offer Darkly his business card next.

Darkly nodded her head.

"Vancouver, too. Alone. I just got out of a relationship. Need to take a break somewhere different."

That would throw him off the scent.

It wasn't untrue. Aaron had been the name of her last boyfriend before her recent undercover assignment. He was a good-looking metro police officer, with a heart of gold, which doomed him from the start.

He had begged Darkly not to end it. He had promised to be there when she needed him, give her space when it was demanded. He'd told her she was the love of his life. Men love to say what's in their heart at any given moment, thinking it will gain them what they want. Nothing could persuade Darkly. The more he pleaded, the easier it was to walk away.

She had woken up one night not long before the breakup and turned to study Aaron's sleeping figure. They'd made love a few hours before. She always hated that term, "made love." Maybe she wasn't a real girl. Afterwards, she had to contend with Aaron's annoying little snore, the way he whimpered when he was unconscious. He suffered from chronic bad dreams, and she realized she really didn't want him there. She couldn't even say she cared deeply for him anymore. Yet, if you'd asked her the day before, she would have been certain of a different answer. Those who didn't know her might think she was incapable of knowing her own mind.

Darkly took a sip of her coffee. Can anyone really trust that the decisions they make are what's best for them? Was she embarking on a fool's quest? Was she leaping out of a plane thinking the clouds would break her fall, not noticing the sharp rocks underneath? The earth has teeth, and it eats us all in time.

The young man offered his hand. "Gus Willet."

Darkly shook his hand firmly. "Darkly Stewart."

"Nice to meet you, Darkly."

Darkly had to admit, Gus was attractive in that surfer, man-boy kind of way.

"Flight 292 to Vancouver, now boarding first class passengers. Those with small children or who require assistance are also free to board at this time."

The announcement brought Darkly back to her senses. Gus hadn't commented on her name. That was strange. Perhaps he was more polite than some. But, she didn't sense any surprise in him. In fact, she got the distinct impression he found exactly what he was looking for. Dad must have sent him.

She watched a young mother push a stroller ahead of her through the gate, while holding a fidgeting child in her other arm. Darkly looked down at her boarding pass and then back at the terminal exit. It wasn't too late. She could get on a plane to somewhere warm and leave her past undiscovered.

Darkly looked down at her hand. The blue veins had faded substantially, thanks to wearing a glove in bed. She made up her mind.

"Is my father flying you first class?"

"Excuse me?"

Despite Gus being a good actor, Darkly recognized her father's handiwork. "No, he's a bargain shopper. Let me see your boarding pass."

Darkly grabbed it out of Gus's hand. A tug-of-war ensued.

"Let me see it."

"Why should I?"

"Because I asked nicely."

The pulling continued, and Gus's grip was slipping.

"Buy me a drink on the plane?" Gus asked.

"I'll buy you a coke," replied Darkly.

"Cokes are free."

"I know."

Darkly won. She read aloud the seat assignment, "14*B*. What do you know, I'm 14*A*."

"Coincidence."

Darkly played her last card. "But we don't believe in coincidences in law enforcement. No one traveling alone willingly chooses a middle seat."

Gus smiled sheepishly and wondered if she was letting him on the plane or was about to cause a fuss that would end with him being escorted off airport premises.

Thirty thousand feet up, the occupants of seats 14A and 14B got to know each other better. Over cokes. With a dash of Jack Daniels.

"So, my father paid for your flight? He and my mum are on a fixed retirement income. I hope that makes you feel good about yourself, Constable."

If Darkly was stuck with Gus for five hours, she was at least going to have some fun torturing him.

"I had vacation time coming. I planned to spend it out west in the Rockies anyway."

Gus took a small sip of his drink.

"The alcohol has a greater effect at this altitude."

"A big strong man like you who protects fragile, young, highly-trained RCMP Constables traveling on their own can surely handle it."

Darkly knocked back her drink in one go.

"And how long did you agree to babysit me?"

"It wasn't like that." Gus sounded genuinely annoyed.

"No?"

"Constable, I've never met your father, but I'm impressed with his style. He called in all his favors on this one. Vincetti assigned me to you. I'm ordered to help you bring back an escaped fugitive. I'm your new partner."

Gus reached his hand out to Darkly. She refused it.

"You can get on a return flight the moment we land. I'll pay."

"That's not going to happen. I'm under orders."

"Some orders shouldn't be obeyed. You can tell my father I said that."

Darkly turned to look out the window. Gus sat back and continued to sip his drink, while Darkly chewed on her nails.

Thirty thousand feet down, a wolf with fur the color of wheat leapt from nearby birch trees into a field of cattle. The wolf had only now stopped to drink after leaving the hospital ten days before. With still more than a week ahead of her, Marielle Bowie needed to feed.

Across the field, on its own, a calf was separated from its mother. Easy prey. As Marielle approached, the prone calf got up and began walking in circles, bellowing for its mother. The mother cow responded and moved quickly across the field. But, Marielle would easily get there first.

The first shot missed its mark. Not again. Marielle had come back from the dead more than once. Firing silver bullets wasn't common practice, after all. Not in the outside world, at least.

Marielle turned back for the birch trees, but the second bullet found its mark, tearing into the left ventricle of her heart. Seconds later, she was dead, just as she was dead when Lawrence fired on her, preventing her from killing Darkly, the heretic. Dead temporarily.

Or so she thought. Marielle did not count on the farmer panicking when he found his cows standing over the naked body of a dead woman. There she lay where he knew in his heart had stood a wolf. How could this have happened? How would he explain this? He would not be able to. And, so, he burned the body, and this time, death remained death.

CHAPTER FIVE

It had seemed like a good idea at the time. Gus and Darkly had taken a Greyhound from the city of Vancouver north to Prince Rupert. Then, they began hitch-hiking east into the vast boreal forest, eventually finding themselves two-thirds of the way to Prince George and a couple days' hike from that little blue dot in the middle of nowhere.

The first day had gone by without incident. On the second day, Darkly and Gus woke in their two-man tent before dawn to the sound of leaves crunching underfoot.

Both reached for their service-issued revolver before a timid female voice called out, "Hello?"

She and a van full of actors were heading to a low-budget horror film shoot about an hour's drive away when they broke down. Serena had spotted the little tent a mile back on the rural country highway and suggested they hike back to ask for help from people who must have a keen sense of how to survive in the wilderness.

Gus was handy with cars, patched the radiator leak with his vinyl tent repair kit, and re-filled the reservoir with water from his canteen.

"It's not hot out. That will last you until the next service station. Where are you headed?"

Jake, the locations manager, as well as camera operator and travel coordinator—meaning driver—answered, "An old gold-rush town. It's not even on the map. Just a little blue dot. 'Wolf Woods,' the locals call it. Tiny place."

Gus and Darkly looked at one another.

"Mind if we hop a lift?" Gus asked.

Darkly conceded with another private glance to Gus that he had proven useful this time. One time was hardly a habit.

The twelve-seat minivan was filled to capacity. Darkly leaned her head on the glass of the passenger window and pretended to doze.

Christopher, the actor playing the serial killer, was in his late 40's, had piercing blue eyes, dressed like an aging rocker, and couldn't stop talking about his time on a Roman Polanski film in Europe. Apparently, Christopher liked younger women, too, as was evidenced by the fact that every time Darkly moved closer to the window, he pressed his leg harder against her own.

The actors were going through their usual first-meeting conversation by reciting their entire resumes and discussing their non-theatrical pastimes, in order to prove to each other and themselves that they were well-rounded individuals. They were not.

Darkly stared out into the thick woods on either side of the highway. She hadn't seen another car for the last fifteen minutes.

Jake hadn't been to Wolf Woods before, but he'd spoken to the sheriff on the phone. The group was going to be an economic jolt in the arm for the town after renting hotel rooms, buying food, and maybe even hiring some local crew.

"Who knows, maybe we'll put them on the map." Jake laughed at his own joke. "Actually, the sheriff's only stipulation was that we don't do that. They're off-the-grid nutballs. You know the type. We had to swear to tell no one where we were going. Northern B.C. That's all anyone knows."

Jake looked out the window at the endless forest.

"We might as well be that plane that went missing in the Indian Ocean."

Peter, whose role was as the hero of the group of camping students being stalked by a backwoods serial killer, called out suddenly, "I see an orange cone!"

Everyone clapped. Jake exhaled a sigh of relief. Christopher patted Darkly's knee.

"I'm happy to put a good word in for you, if you'd like a role. I'm an acting coach, too, you know."

Darkly looked in Gus's direction, opening her eyes wide. If he wanted to show her how useful he could be, now was another one of those ideal moments.

Gus was enjoying watching Darkly squirm and decided to encourage Christopher further.

"I think that's a great idea. She's such a ham. She'd be perfect. Don't let me get in the way of your dreams, hon."

Darkly and Gus had agreed that, as far as the film folk were concerned, they were a couple.

Next to the cone, a staked, cardboard sign read, "Wolf Woods... 5km." Jake pulled the van up next to the sign. Taped to the cone was a rain-smudged note. Peter opened the side door and leapt out.

"I'll take a look."

"Looks like the hero is already getting into character," Christopher said and winked at Serena on the other side of him.

Peter pulled the note off the cone and held it up to the sun. Then, he crumpled it into a ball and threw it into the woods.

Shane, the first actor to die in the script, yelled out the window, "Litterbug!"

Peter walked back to the van. Suddenly, there was tremendous commotion in the woods where Peter had thrown the paper. The trees shook violently, and there was the noise of snapping branches.

"Shit!"

Peter ran the last couple strides to the van, leapt in, and slammed the door behind him.

Everyone pressed their faces to the glass on Darkly's side of the van. Christopher was breathing down her neck. Darkly thought she saw something move: a sleek, brown flash across a break in the bushes. Darkly poked Gus.

"Did you see that?"

"What?"

"I don't know."

The forest went quiet, except for the call of a far-off bird.

Jake broke the silence. "It was a moose." When all else fails, blame the moose. It's the B.C. way. "What did the note say?"

Peter was still catching his breath, when all eyes turned to him.

"Damn. I thought I was going to have a heart attack. Um, the turn-off is just ahead on the right," Peter finally revealed.

Jake drove about another fifty feet and turned down a gravel road, which was marked by another orange cone. On either side, at the edge of the woods, large logs lay in piles. To Darkly's pleasure, Christopher hit his head on the roof when the van's tires fell victim to the troughs left by the logs being dragged clear of the road.

The minivan followed the winding and hilly road up to a steep incline. The van groaned, and Jake slipped the transmission into second gear for the climb to the top of the slope.

"Come on, baby, just a little farther. Don't overheat on me now."

The van did successfully break through the tree line onto a large bluff. Ahead of the cast, was the film's circus: a pick-up truck, a couple of RVs, and a generator that powered the camp.

The First Assistant Director came out of one of the RVs and waved his arms at Jake.

"That's the First AD, and the only AD, as well as Catering Manager, Wardrobe, and Props Master," Jake explained.

"Is he makeup, too?" Serena asked Jake.

"You'll be doing your own makeup on this one."

Serena shook her head. This deal was getting worse by the minute.

The van pulled up in front of a wooden barrier at the edge of the bluff. The actors piled out. Christopher offered his hand to Darkly, and at the last minute, grabbed her around the waist to lower her down to the ground.

"Strong like bull." He beat his chest for effect.

Christopher then joined Serena, Shane, Peter, and Gus in hunting for a porta-john.

Darkly walked up to the barrier and looked down at the valley below and the little town of Wolf Woods. An old 1970s GMC truck drove along the main street. A few people were milling about their front yards and store fronts.

Darkly took out her smart phone and snapped a photo of the valley.

"You want me to take a photo of you?"

Darkly turned around to face the First AD.

"Name's Marvin."

Marvin was a nice, clean-cut guy. He was very enthusiastic, which meant he was new to the game and had no clue what abuse he was going to undergo at the hands of everyone else on set. If there was a problem, he would be the one expected to fix it.

Marvin was wearing shorts, and Darkly could see from the welts all over his legs that the mosquitoes were bad around here. Marvin followed Darkly's gaze.

"Oh, I have a bug zapper paddle if you need it. And spray. They don't generally come out till dusk. And to be honest, I seem to be the only one they really like. Would you like to see your trailer?"

"Oh, I'm not -"

"Serena?"

"No." Darkly waved her hand in the van's direction. "We just hopped a lift."

"Ah. I get it now. Well, if you're staying in town overnight, there's a hotel. Doesn't look like it's been renovated in fifty years, but it's clean. Ish."

Gus scoped out the scene on the way back from the toilet-in-a-box. A sign that read "Star Trailer" was taped to the side of one of the campers. The custom-renovated RV was divided into two compartments, and there was a door to each compartment. Serena's name was posted on one of the doors, Peter's on the other. Gus watched Serena climb the little metal steps up to her half of the trailer. She looked back and gave Gus a smile.

Marvin called out to her, "Craft services is just on the other side of the circus, if you want a coffee or anything?"

Serena disappeared inside without answering, but Gus thought he could do with a caffeine jolt.

"Thanks, I could use some coffee," Gus replied.

Gus returned to Darkly's side and shook Marvin's hand.

"Then I think we should head down into town, right, hon?"

Darkly wasn't liking the profuse use of Gus's chosen term of endearment for her. She nodded her head with contempt.

"Think one of your boys could give us a lift? Down there?" Gus asked Marvin.

Marvin stammered, looking for a way to say no to Gus without appearing rude. He had a helluva lot to do.

"Seeing as we fixed your van, got your actors here," Gus pressed.

"Oh, right. Thank you. Sure. I'll drop you both off myself." Marvin tapped the outlook railing. "Wait here for me. I just have to get the talent settled in."

"Thank you, Marvin," Darkly said in her most flirtatious voice.

She touched Marvin's arm lightly, and the bespectacled kid in his early twenties melted.

Finally, it was quiet. Serena could hear herself think for the first time since she was standing in her shower at three this morning. She looked around the trailer. It was a nice size. There was a toilet at one end, which she wished she had been told of before entering that fly-infested portable septic tank. Across from the toilet, there was a small kitchenette with a counter, beer fridge, and sink. She peered out the little window above the sink and watched Peter and Shane laughing beside the craft services table.

Serena popped her second colloidal silver pill of the day. The actress swore by it to protect her against all matter of infection. No doubt she swore by her breast implants, as well.

Darkly took a long hard look at the town below. The placement of buildings was vaguely familiar to her. She looked to the left of the center of town, where she expected to see a church steeple, and there it was.

Gus followed Darkly's gaze.

"So, there's this fugitive. She's wanted for trafficking young women." Gus was relaying the facts back to Darkly.

"I think this one's hunting men," Darkly corrected him.

"You sure?"

"I've seen her in action. She preys on men with low self-esteem."

"Wow. These actors better watch their step then. Narcissism and low self-worth go hand in hand."

"I think Christopher would ask her where to sign up. Thanks for helping me out with him in the van, by the way. I don't think she'd be Shane and Peter's type. Look at this town, Gus. Only one road to the outside world, situated at the bottom of the valley, not listed on most maps, and no way to physically see it unless you're looking down on it from above. You get kidnapped and brought here, no one's going to find you."

Darkly looked back at the two actors, Shane and Peter, now making their way to their trailers.

"No one knows they're here," Darkly continued. "The sheriff himself told them to keep it a secret."

"Holy Christ, Darkly. What sort of place have you brought me to?" asked Gus.

Darkly pulled out her smart phone. No bars.

"To a place where no one can hear you call for help," she replied.

CHAPTER SIX

Sheriff Buckwald Robertson opened the chamber of his 1972 police-issued handgun and placed a single bullet inside. His friends, or those who thought of him as a friend, called him Buck. He personally didn't think of most people as friends. There was a difference in having your fate tied to people and liking them.

Doc Ross shook his head.

"You're a piece of work, Buck. What's she gonna do now?"

"I'm not questioning your abilities as a medicine man, Doc. This town expects me to take precautions. I'll live with your disapproval, if it means I'm doing my job right."

"She's seventeen. She'll grow out of it. And if you're going to shoot her, give me a little warning so I can step back."

Doc winked at the teenager sitting on the examination table in front of him.

"No one grows out of it completely," said Buck knowingly.

Buck never winked at anyone in his life. Nor did he find anything charming. Ever.

Victoria looked coyly at Buck.

"You'd shoot your girlfriend's only child, Sheriff?"

Buck's expression was as void of emotion as a stone.

"We were over before you were born."

Victoria winced as Doc poured whisky over a deep cut on her arm.

"A waste of good whisky."

That might have been the hint of a smile on Buck's face, if he ever actually smiled.

"I wouldn't have to waste it, if your boy could steal me some rubbing alcohol. Maybe those movie people have a first aid kit. Well," he paused, "Victoria, that's the best I can do under these conditions. You'll heal without the stitches. Good thing, too, as I'm all out of cat gut."

Doc shook his head in frustration.

"Wash the wounds thoroughly a couple times a day and let the air get to them at night."

Doc pulled a set of keys from his pocket and unlocked the door of an antique wood and glass chemist's cabinet. He pulled out a brown glass bottle full of pills and passed it to the girl.

"Take two of these just before bed next time you feel a little anxious. You are guaranteed to not wake up for eight hours. Hell, an elephant wouldn't wake up for seven."

"Do you have a pair of scissors?" Victoria asked Doc.

Victoria jumped off the examination table. Its leather padding had been sewn up innumerable times, and stuffing was poking out of the corners.

Doc Ross opened a drawer next to the medicine cabinet, pulled out a pair of stainless steel scissors and handed them to Victoria. He then had second thoughts about it, and a battle appeared likely.

"I need a haircut." Victoria wasn't letting go.

Doc gave in, and Buck frowned. Victoria walked over to a mirror on the examining room wall and began cutting out chunks of hair. Clumps of tangled, chestnut brown hair filled with nettles and dirt fell to the floor.

Buck walked up close to Doc and whispered, "And when you run out of pills?"

"Why don't you go give one of those Hollywood actors a ticket for littering, Buck."

"I didn't hurt anyone," Victoria shot in Buck's direction.

"So you say," said Buck as he left Doc's office. He had other work to do.

Victoria looked at the reflection of her shorn hair in the mirror. There wasn't a strand left that was the same length.

Doc put his hand on Victoria's shoulder. "It will look fine after you wash it. I'm told short hair on ladies is in fashion now."

"What *do* I do when I run out of pills?"

"I'll get more."

"That's a little hard when you don't actually have a license to practice medicine, isn't it?" Victoria looked at herself in the mirror again. "I'll grow out it."

Doc turned his back on Victoria and said coldly, "Make sure you do, or I'll put you down myself."

Buck walked into the Moon River Diner and sat down at the counter. An attractive woman in her late thirties placed a coffee cup down in front of the sheriff and filled it. A feint scar ran down the woman's left cheek.

"How is she?"

Buck grabbed the woman's arm and pulled her face in close to his. A wooden cross fell out of Geraldine's cleavage and swung back and forth in front of Buck.

Momentarily, he was lost to another time. Seventeen years previous to be exact.

The ticking of the Westminster clock accompanied the beading of sweat on the upper lip of a woman fighting for what she believed was her own salvation. Her corneas were turning yellow, and the blood pooling under her nails was seeping onto the white sheets. She tried to pray, but her vocal chords no longer worked.

"Come on, sweetheart. It doesn't have to be this hard."

A much younger Geraldine held Catharine's hand. Geraldine wasn't thrilled about helping the woman who despised her and all who were like her. But if Catherine was important to Buck, then Geraldine must make an effort. Perhaps she would win Buck's affections yet.

Outside the cabin, the growling and scratching at the door was frantic. Buck looked back at Geraldine, resignation in his eyes.

"At this rate, they'll kill us all."

He tossed the kitchen chairs out of his way like kindling and grabbed hold of the heavy oak table that dominated the cabin's main room. He dragged it to the door and grunted as he overturned it.

Catharine's condition was becoming more desperate. As well as breathing heavily, she was now snarling. Saliva was dripping from her mouth, and her nails had become as sharp and long as talons. But she was still fighting it. Geraldine could see that in Catharine's eyes. Nature was still not guaranteed to win. The black hair on Catharine's head was spreading out onto the bed like ivy. She reached out her hand toward Buck.

It was Geraldine who called to him. "Buck!"

Buck took another look at the door. It would hold for now. He went to Catharine's side.

Catharine grabbed Buck's arm and dug her nails deep into his flesh. He didn't pull away. The muscles on her arm were taut and well-defined. At this moment, she was stronger than he was, and Buck knew there wasn't much time left.

"Let go. Please. Just let it happen. For the sake of your son."

He tried to sound comforting. But, the man on the other side of that door, his brother, had killed their father and had now come for him.

Catharine found the strength to plead with her voice one final time. "Do it."

The words were tormented whispers, but they tore through Buck's spine like the most piercing of screams. He looked down at his gun holster.

"Buck, what are you doing?"

Geraldine had had enough of both of their games. She placed her hand over her extended belly. Her husband had been banished, so she had taken a stand with Buck. Now that same husband would take revenge on her. His unborn child would not save her. This was a classic grab for power, and the man outside was prepared to accept his own losses as part of the devil's bargain.

Buck removed the gun from its holster. Geraldine let go of Catharine's hand.

"Buck. No."

Catharine smiled and nodded her head with difficulty. She let go of Buck's arm. Her head sank back into her pillow, and she panted softly.

Catharine wished to die on her own terms, if not free of the curse, at least in the way and form she chose. Geraldine did not know how Catharine remained alive. Their kind must change at least once during a moon's cycle. To have fought nature in this way through sheer willpower, for three cycles, was unchartered territory.

Buck's hands shook, as he loaded one silver bullet after another into the gun.

But Buck didn't finish off the suffering woman in his bed. No. Instead, he got up and walked over to a bassinet, where his adopted son was soundly sleeping, oblivious to the deliverers of death at the door.

Buck took the safety off the gun and pointed it at the child. At Catharine's little boy, Trey.

Catharine turned her head and opened her eyes. Her panting became ferocious in its speed, met by the splintering of wood at the front door. As an intelligent woman, her reasoning told her that, in death, her son would be spared a painful life. As a mother faced with her child's immediate demise, her instinct had other ideas.

Buck was now completely calm in his resolve. "If they make it through that door, your son is dead. I can't shoot them all. If you won't turn, not even for him, then I will be the one to end his short life. Not them."

Buck knew that his brother's followers numbered maybe seven or eight at the most. They were young, inexperienced. They drew their strength from their leader. They rallied to him as to a king. Kill him, and their loyalty to one another would collapse. So, there was a small chance.

Catharine's eyes turned from yellow to red. Buck and Geraldine alone would be overpowered. But, if Catharine turned, if she gave up this silly notion of noble suicide, their odds would improve.

What legend said about a mother wolf protecting her cub was an understatement. Legend had no idea.

"You never could handle that girl. You coddled her from day one, never acted in her best interests." Buck was back in the present in the diner.

"You didn't help me any."

"I took her to Doc. Doc gave her drugs."

"That's it, then. It's under control."

Geraldine returned the glass coffee carafe to its stand.

"No, she's out of control, Geraldine. It's a band-aid. Did you see Ed's dog? Did you see him? She's just like her father."

"Why is it always 'her father' or 'your husband?' He was *your* brother."

"You made your choice."

"Yes, I did. I chose to stand with you."

Geraldine broke loose of Buck's grip.

"You'd think seventeen years would be enough time to get over the rest. It would be for any other man, Buck. You're too sensitive."

Buck ignored the remark.

"The coffee's cold."

"The heating pad finally gave out. It's going to be cold more often than hot."

"Victoria needs to be brought into line, forced if necessary. Or she's lost."

Geraldine leveled her eyes at Buck.

"What are you saying, Buck? She needs a husband to beat it out of her? Break her so she takes her proper place?"

"Ed said he'd help you out, as payment for his injury and his dog."

Geraldine bristled. "That's the cost of a dowry these days? A fucking mutt? You tell that filthy redneck farmer that if he ever touches my daughter, I'll bite his other ear off. You know well enough that Vicky has eyes for only one boy."

Buck went stiff.

"Keep that girl away from my son."

"Or what?"

Geraldine fought the urge to back down and shut up. Buck and she had been through a lot together. She knew talking always made their situation worse. What was it the outside world called it? Communication? They could keep it.

Buck looked at Geraldine and shook his head. "Don't."

Geraldine softened. "You're a good man, Buck. I know you've been protecting her in your own way. Don't think I haven't noticed. Don't think I'm not grateful."

Geraldine put her hand on Buck's.

"I'd sure like it if you let me say thank you every once in a while. I *need* to say thank you. You need it. What man doesn't?"

Buck pulled his hand free and took a sip of his cold coffee.

Geraldine directed her words at Buck so only he could hear them. "How many years do I have to pay you penance?"

At that moment, an old man with a tobacco-stained beard walked into the diner carrying a pail full of rags. He put the bucket down next to the coat rack by the entrance and hung his hat.

Geraldine hit a bell on the order window counter a little too hard. How many times had she taken out her frustrations on that damn thing? It never broke. She wouldn't be broken either.

Geraldine yelled to the cook, "Hash!"

The old man made his way over to a stool in front of Geraldine.

"Those windows are mighty dirty today. It's the warm wind. Dust blowing off the mountains."

Geraldine placed a clean coffee mug down on the counter.

"How 'bout we include a slice of pie today, Jasper?"

Jasper plopped himself down in front of Geraldine, as she poured him a coffee.

"Oh? Well now, I suppose that would be fine, Geraldine. Don't need to watch my waistline at my age."

Jasper looked out the dirty diner windows.

"The light is going, though. I'll probably have to come back tomorrow to finish the job. Yep, definitely a two-day job."

Geraldine smiled and nodded her head. Jasper reached for a small sugar bowl and spooned several heaping teaspoons into his black coffee. He then picked up his mug and examined it.

"This mug's chipped."

"They're all chipped, Jasper."

It was Buck who pointed that fact out, and Jasper glanced over at the sheriff.

"Afternoon, Sheriff. You been up to see those movie people yet?"

Geraldine laid a large plate of corned beef hash and a bottle of ketchup in front of Jasper.

"They're coming in here tonight for a meal," said Geraldine.

Jasper opened the ketchup and pounded the bottom of the bottle with his palm. The sweet red paste hit his hash in splatters that spilled over onto the counter.

"That so? How long they staying with us?"

Geraldine grabbed the ketchup bottle out of Jasper's hands.

"This stuff don't grow on trees."

"I heard it's five weeks," Jasper said unfazed.

Buck didn't reply.

"I'll bet it's longer," Jasper mused.

Jasper turned back to his plate of hash and began shoveling it into his mouth.

"Can't think of the last time I went to the pictures. Something with Mary Pickford, I think. That was a classy fox," Jasper reminisced through his mouthful.

CHAPTER SEVEN

What was that thumping? It wouldn't stop. Serena came to. She'd fallen asleep in a crooked position on the tiny RV couch. The trailer cabinets rattled, as the thumping resumed.

"Serena?" A vaguely familiar voice called out. "It's Carter. The director. We spoke briefly on the phone."

Serena's agent had given her the low-down on this guy. Thirty-something, but not exactly the latest wunderkind to come out of Hollywood. He was a trust fund baby still living off his parents' talents. Every business Daddy set up for him collapsed within a couple years. None of it involved any kind of hard work, of course. There was the baseball team that was demoted from Triple A to just A; completely skipping a division. Or was that called minor league? Serena didn't know anything about sports. There was the deep sea fishing business. Two boats sank in rough water. Carter was pulled out of the ocean by the coast guard. That one made the front page of the Miami Herald at least.

But when Carter showed up on a list of suckers who Bernie Madoff had pursued real estate ventures with, Daddy put his wallet away. Carter eventually convinced his father to give him one more shot, and so he set out to become an independent filmmaker. He was going to prove his worth to his father once and for all by sinking his last penny into a business where the first rule of thumb is "never use your own money." Well, technically, he was using Daddy's money.

Serena sat up. Her back went into spasms, causing her to hunch over. She'd sleep on the floor before suffering this couch again. She straightened herself up, put on a smile, and opened the door.

"Carter!" She extended her hand. "It's great to meet you. Thank you so much for this opportunity."

Carter was average height, average weight, and average looks. His nervous smile belied an unwavering conviction that the eventual outcome would make up for the road full of potholes he drove down to get there.

"How's your home away from home?" He looked around. "Comfortable? You have a sink. I don't have one of those. My office is the pickup."

This was bound to be the obligatory bonding session, where Serena was supposed to ask the director what the character was actually *feeling* while being chased topless through the woods by a serial killer. Peter and Shane had already placed a bet with her that Carter would use the words "female empowerment," "overcoming the odds," and "I don't want you to do anything that makes you feel uncomfortable" at least once during their conversation.

Carter stepped into the RV.

"I thought I could share with you my whole vision thing. The short version."

Carter looked away to his left a little. Where had Serena read that was an indication the person was being dishonest about something?

"Uh, your agent told you about the, uh, situation?"

"You mean the non-union thing or showing my boobs?"

"Oh. I don't want you to feel uncomfortable in any way. It will be a closed set."

"Yeah, my agent told me I'd probably lose my union status, but she needs the money, and I'm leaving for L.A. the moment I'm done filming. I'm not coming back."

"I see."

"Yeah. I've lived through enough snow for one lifetime."

"Well, the snow's all melted here, and the town's been really good about welcoming us. No permits for filming. They're just happy to get a boost to their local economy. My GPS couldn't even find this place. It's like a modern-day Brigadoon." He wrapped up, "Okay then, I have to say hello to the other actors. We'll see each other at the cast meal tonight. I don't know what they have to eat around here. Probably moose burgers or something like that. Oh, sorry, you're not vegetarian, are you?"

"I eat fish. That's a pescatarian. What about the vision?"

"Vision?"

"Your vision. You were going to enlighten me."

"Oh, right."

This guy wasn't Spielberg.

"Well, I don't see it as a slasher movie, and you aren't a victim. These students find the strength within themselves to overcome the terrible odds that are stacked against their very survival."

Bingo. Serena stifled a laugh, even though she'd just lost a fiver each to Peter and Shane.

"That's exactly how I saw it when I read the script."

"Cool. Really?"

"Oh yeah."

Serena wondered how many gallons of fake blood Carter had ordered, and how much of it would end up being poured on her breasts.

Carter smiled and said goodbye to Serena's chest.

On the way out of Serena's trailer, Carter caught sight of Darkly and Gus still sitting by the edge of the overlook. Marvin had gotten them a couple chairs, which they looked up from as Carter's head blocked their sun. Gus snapped surveillance photos of the town with his Nikon 35mm camera.

"Hi. I'm Carter. The Director. I understand you helped my director of photography out of a bind. Nice camera."

It had been a couple of days since Darkly and Gus had enjoyed anything more than granola bars, so they accepted the invite to the cast and crew meal. In fact, Gus had found his way onto the crew as their stills photographer, making Darkly his assistant.

Darkly sat next to Marvin at The Moon River Diner. Serena was on the other side of her popping pills, and Christopher was next to Serena. The most he was able to do from that position was play footsie with Darkly, which was better than rubbing her knee.

Carter gave them all his mission statement and thanked the diner owner, Geraldine, for handling the cast and crew meals. She was also one of two waitresses, the dishwasher, and the cook when the other cook was sleeping off a bottle of moonshine.

Sheriff Buck gave everyone a lecture about the dangers of local wildlife, rock slides, and rough water.

Serena had a hard time keeping her lower lip connected to her upper lip in front of Buck. He was clearly a looker. That's what Darkly's grandmother would have called him. His hair was an unusual bluish silver, which hung down over his ears. His eyes were the color of steel. Where one expected his skin to be leathered to match the mature shade of hair, his face was, instead, boyish and taut. No sign of crow's feet on this man in his late thirties, though there was the permanent scowl on his face.

Geraldine gave a small talk on The Moon River Diner: how the wife of a Gold Rush miner had fed every young man who headed west to build the railway and how her family had restored the place to its former glory.

That couldn't have been terribly glorious by Darkly's assessment. The Formica tables had coffee ring stains that had to date back to the 1950s. The seats of the chairs were covered in enough duct tape to wrap around the planet at least once. The whole town appeared in dire need of a team of handymen and interior designers.

The meal was actually quite good. They started with wild leek and mushroom soup, which Geraldine's daughter, Victoria, spilled all over Christopher. It must be quite intimidating for a teenage girl secluded in the middle of nowhere to have Hollywood come to town.

Peter and Shane were both former waiters and jumped in to help pass the rest of the soup around and then the venison cutlets and boar sausages. The bread pudding was pretty much the best thing Darkly had ever eaten.

It was over coffee that Darkly noticed a curl of smoke wafting past the window. She was gagging for a cigarette. She excused herself and headed for the toilets. At the Ladies, she kept going and slipped out the back exit.

The night air was warm, and a wind was blowing. The tiny lights of the circus trailers up on the hill above the town were reflected in the Moon River. She smelled the cigarette, then saw the flicker of red over by the diner's grease pit.

"Can you spare one of those?"

Victoria emerged into the faint beam of the back door's overhead incandescent light bulb. She held a pack of American Spirits out to Darkly.

Darkly took one out and put it in her mouth. Victoria tossed her black metal lighter to Darkly. Darkly ignited the flame and smiled at Victoria.

"I love the smell of butane in the evening."

Victoria stared blankly back.

"Sorry. Bad joke. The movie. Apocalypse Now."

"Never saw it."

Darkly inhaled deeply and shoved the lighter into her pocket out of habit.

"Thanks. I needed that. My name's Darkly."

Victoria took another drag on her own cigarette and then gave up her own name. "Victoria."

"That's a pretty name. Not like mine."

"I never liked it."

Darkly decided to start fishing. "I'm guessing you don't get many visitors to this town."

"I gotta meet my boyfriend now."

Victoria threw her cigarette butt to the ground and walked back into the diner.

Darkly called after her, "Come and visit us on set if you like. My boyfriend is the photographer."

No answer back.

"Or not."

Darkly took a final drag herself and turned back to the exit. Geraldine was standing there waiting for her.

"I'm sorry. I didn't hear the door open."

"She will have stolen those cigarettes off one of your friends."

"Oh, right."

Darkly looked down at the half-finished cigarette in her hand.

"I guess I shouldn't have encouraged her."

"She's going through a rebellious stage." Geraldine held open the exit door. "Everyone's leaving. Sheriff's giving you a lift to the hotel."

"That's okay. You know, I think I'll just walk. It's warm out."

Geraldine nodded and went back inside.

"Mothers everywhere just love me," Darkly said sarcastically to herself.

Darkly dropped the cigarette and crushed it into the gravel with her boot.

The back of Buck's pickup accommodated the cast members, while Marvin drove Carter back to the circus. The crew was camping out in tents to save money. Christopher patted down his clothes, looking for something.

"Damn, I must have left my cigs at the circus."

Buck pulled up next to Darkly and Geraldine. He leaned out the driver's window.

"You sure you don't want a ride? Hotel's on the other side of town."

"No thanks, Sheriff, I like walking at night."

Buck looked at Geraldine. She rolled her eyes for dramatic effect.

"I'll see to it she gets there alive, Buck."

"You do that. Bears are bad this time of year. Eating out of people's trash cans. Where's Victoria?"

"You mean, who's she with?" She patted Buck's arm. "You know full well."

Next to Buck, on the passenger side of the cab's bench seat, Gus lifted up his camera to show Darkly.

"I'll get some video footage of the town. For the DVD extras. Honey."

Buck pulled his arm in the truck and drove away, dislodging Christopher's perch on the wheel hub. He landed in Serena's lap. Darkly could hear Christopher leering, if such a thing was possible, as he apologized with the help of his roaming hands.

"Sorry about that, love."

Geraldine put her arm through Darkly's. "I want you to call me Gerri. Let's walk along the river, shall we? Believe it or not, you are not the first Darkly I've met. Did you like the meal?"

"It was great. The venison was the most delicious meat I've ever eaten."

"Well, the folks of Wolf Woods know how to bring down a deer from an early age."

The two set off. Darkly felt an immediate connection to Gerri. The older woman's red hairs had faded, but would have been a rich strawberry blond in her youth.

"You've known him long?" Darkly asked.

Geraldine's eyes were glued to the crescent moon when she replied, "Who, Buck? All my life."

"I guess that was a dumb question in such a small place. Is he always so light-hearted?"

"Oh, Buck's just Buck. Some people are born grumps, I guess."

Geraldine led Darkly into a back yard and past the hum of a generator.

"We get our electricity in town from kerosene generators. Black-outs are pretty common in the winter when the roads are blocked. Not much makes it into town when the roads are blocked. Everything you ate tonight is local."

Gerri opened a wooden gate in a crumbling brick wall overrun with vines pushing their way through the mortar. Darkly passed through the wall to find herself standing on a narrow slope that fell down to the gently-flowing river below. Darkly hoped she could hear the calming sound of shallow water flowing over rock from her hotel window.

"So, Victoria's your daughter. What does your husband do?"

"He died a long time ago."

"I'm sorry."

Darkly and Geraldine strolled past manicured lawns behind small clapboard homes.

"Buck's the closest thing to a father Victoria ever had. And a pretty sorry excuse for one, at that. Buck was Wyatt, my husband's, brother."

Darkly sensed she had opened a wound. But, there was something else. Geraldine was holding back her emotions, keeping herself in check, binding her thoughts. Darkly likened it to smelling blood underwater.

"Sorry if I brought back a bad memory."

"You can't stop that around here. Every day is filled by the memory of something in a small town. And everyone has a different account of the same memory to tell."

"Do you mind if I ask how your husband died?"

"Hunting accident. We have a lot of hunting accidents around here."

"I guess I should wear an orange vest if I ever take a hike."

Geraldine stopped and gripped Darkly's arm more tightly. "Don't you go hiking alone in these woods, you hear me?" Geraldine let go of Darkly's arm. "The bears," she added almost as an afterthought.

Darkly recognized more than concern in Geraldine's face. There was genuine fear. But, again, the fear seemed misplaced. It was fear for what was in the woods, not Darkly.

"Okay," she whispered.

"Sorry. Buck has a habit of setting me on edge, is all. He and I have a history. I left him for his brother, and he never forgave me."

"Some people can't let things go, I guess."

Darkly doubted that was of any comfort, but she felt the need to say something. A small cloud bank rolled in, covering the moon. The night became suddenly darker. Much darker. Darkly looked up to see the clear section of sky awash with the Milky Way.

"Wow, you don't see that in the city."

"You have your own spectacular light show, I suspect. Makes you feel small, doesn't it? Like everything we worry about down here means absolutely nothing."

"An ex-boyfriend of mine used to say we're ants building a hill out of dirt that's just going to get washed away by a cosmic flood."

Geraldine smiled. "So, you're attracted to cynics too, huh?"

"Oh, Aaron wasn't a cynic. He was a romantic. He put all his faith in me and had little left for anything else."

"Darling, that is pretty much the definition of a cynic. They find it almost impossible to see beauty in the world, so they attach their obsessive search for it on one thing. And that one thing becomes their savior or downfall."

"Are we talking about Buck?"

Geraldine sighed. "Buck is the best man I ever knew. Loyal to a fault, unswerving in his duty to protect everything that falls within his responsibility and beyond. He is the definition of a man. I thought to myself many moons ago, 'That is the kind of fella you grab hold of and never let go. He'll keep you safe, and you will feel loved with an unflinching power, until the day you die.' So, when I was nineteen and he finally asked me out, I decided that was it. I was going to marry him."

Geraldine and Darkly approached a steep road that ended abruptly at a ford in the river. The road picked up again on the other side.

"Hotel's up here. It's great exercise."

Geraldine and Darkly began to climb the steep road, and Geraldine continued the story of her past.

"For Buck, life is a constant. He's still living the same day now two decades gone. But, for most of us, life is a series of circumstances that are unplanned. It was here where we're standing that it happened. I was walking home from the diner. I was a waitress then too. I saw Buck's older brother take off all his clothes and walk into the water for a swim. He was a beautiful man. Long hair. *Perrrfect* body."

Geraldine had drawn out the word "perfect" for Darkly to get the message.

Darkly piped up. "In case you didn't notice, the sheriff's pretty gorgeous."

Geraldine leaned in close to Darkly. "Wyatt was gorgeous and dangerous. He rode a motorcycle! He was a man to be tamed who had broken many a heart. Wyatt would disappear into the woods for days and bring back a wild boar draped over the broadest shoulders you'd ever seen," Geraldine remembered. "Well, he saw me and asked me to come in for a dip. I have no clue what possessed me to do it. But, I just couldn't say no to that boy. We swam to the other side of the river, where he told me he had always loved me. He said, if he couldn't be with me, he would leave town and never come back. There were many girls who couldn't hold on to him, and here he was saying he belonged to me. I knew if he really did leave, I'd follow closely behind. And nobody leaves Wolf Woods."

Geraldine looked up the hill. There was still a distance to go.

"We should make a move on up. This ain't New York City. Lewis will lock the door to the hotel and go to bed. And you don't want to spend a night on my couch getting stabbed by rusty springs."

"Not until you tell me the end of the story."

Geraldine shook her head. "I know now that there's nothing romantic about tragedy. Victoria was conceived that night. Wyatt and I were married six weeks later. A month after that, he was killed on a hunting trip. Buck refused to go to the funeral."

"That's awful. Wyatt was his brother. And he was dead!"

"Wyatt would have understood. He said to me once, 'For what I've done to him, Buck and I are no longer brothers and never will be again.' Wyatt knew better than anyone how his brother saw the world, and he always envied the fact that Buck was a better man than he was."

"So, Victoria never met her father."

Geraldine's voice became a little choked up. "I went to Buck just days before Victoria was born and asked him to marry me. I told him I still had feelings for him and that I would do anything he needed to be a good wife to him. I wanted Victoria to be raised as his daughter."

"And he said no?"

Darkly actually felt an emotion welling up from somewhere. The story had impacted her like she was connected to these people who tortured themselves.

Geraldine nodded. "The worst part is, that moment made me realize I really was in love with him. In the course of nine months, I lost the only two men I ever cared for."

Geraldine stopped in front of a three-story brick building. A weather-worn sign on the front read "The Royal Tavern and Inn."

"Oh well," Geraldine exhaled, "Don't go getting wrapped up in my drama. It doesn't do any good to revisit your own past, let alone someone else's."

"So he spent all these years bitter and alone because of his pride? Men."

Darkly suspected there was more to this story than just love and betrayal. Or maybe not. Maybe love and betrayal summed up just about all possible outcomes to any story.

Geraldine laughed a little and wiped the water from her eyes.

"Oh, he wasn't alone for long. And she gave him an amazing boy. Trey has the best qualities of both Buck and Wyatt, if you ask me. It's no wonder my daughter loves him."

The hotel owner, Lewis Bowie, was a slight man with a comb-over so sparse, he was, in essence, bald. He looked annoyed to have waited up so long for Darkly to arrive. She wondered why he wasn't jumping for joy. Despite the odd husband being locked out of his home for drinking at the bar too late, she couldn't imagine the place spilling over with bookings.

The corridor of rooms was dimly lit by a small table-top lamp at one end of a row of doors. Lewis slipped a key into the door knob below a brass number plate that read "ROOM 209." The door opened with a loud creek into a darkened room.

"Bathroom's directly across the hall." He pointed to the door a few feet away from Darkly's room. "Good night."

"Where's my friend?"

Lewis handed Darkly the key.

"Down the hall."

That didn't exactly answer the question. Lewis turned and walked back down the hallway. Then, he remembered something and turned to speak at Darkly again.

"My niece, Marielle, changes the bedding, but she's away at the moment. So -" He left it at that.

Darkly stood in the hallway in a daze for a minute. Could Lewis's niece and her Marielle be one in the same? She'd certainly wait around for Marielle's return to find out.

Darkly felt for the light switch on the inside wall of her room and flipped it up. Nothing. She could make out an outline of a dresser and slid cautiously along what felt like a hardwood floor to the edge of the unit. She slid her hand along the wooden surface until she felt a lamp. She ran her fingers up the neck and pushed the switch.

The bed was a twin size and had a worn red comforter draped across it that was too big and gathered in rolls on the floor. Darkly made a depression in the bed with her hand. Geraldine's infamous couch couldn't feel much worse. At least the lamp was dim enough that the mildew stains covering the ceiling were barely noticeable in the shadows. She was sure that would change with the morning light.

Darkly went to the window and pulled back the lace curtains. A small puff of dust stirred. She reached over a couple of dead flies on the sill and pulled up on the window. Was it nailed in place? It clearly hadn't been opened in a long time. With a couple deep breaths and by putting some muscle into it, Darkly managed to lift the window halfway up the frame.

She blew the fly carcasses out into the night air and, in doing so, granted them their last wish posthumously. She leaned her head out to escape the dank air inside.

She had a view of the river and could make out the shallow part where Geraldine and she had turned to climb the hill. There was no sight of Geraldine now. Just the shadow of a large dog walking along the riverside, where she had stepped twenty or so minutes before. Geraldine had disappeared, just like every other living soul in the town. She looked at her watch. Eleven. That was when The Senate was getting busy. This really was a ghost town.

Darkly couldn't hear the water from this distance, but she could make out the opposite bank of the river under the once more revealed moonlight. She looked at the bank of thick grass and imagined Wyatt and Geraldine lying naked on the ground. She could see it all in her mind. Wyatt was kissing Geraldine on her face, her arms, her legs, then running his hand expectantly down over her stomach, and finally climbing on top of her.

Darkly thought about Gus. She imagined his hands pinning her wrists to the bed, feeling his entire weight on top of her, and their breathing quickening together until she was overcome with the light-headed sensation that started a chain reaction that traveled all the way to her core. Then she thought about the sheriff. She imagined him standing in front of her at the end of the bed right now wanting her. What the hell was she doing here?

CHAPTER EIGHT

Darkly opened her eyes and looked up at the ceiling. It was just as she imagined. Different stains of mildew: black, yellow, brown, red. Red? That couldn't be healthy. All of them were in patches that spread out from the corners of the room, hopping over clear patches in the center of the ceiling. She looked to either side of the bed. There was no clock.

"What time is it?" she thought aloud.

Darkly reached down next to the bed into a pile of her clothes she'd stripped off. She felt around until she found her phone. It was dead. She looked outside and gauged it was shortly after six. Yes, RCMP officers were still required to know what time it was without a timepiece.

There was already another fly carcass on the sill. She could only make out the roof of the hardware store across the road. Darkly flopped back on her dusty pillow and resigned herself to another ten minutes of sleep.

"Darkly."

There was a knock.

"Darkly, it's Gus. You up yet?"

Darkly called out it in that voice she had used countless school mornings to placate Elizabeth. "I'm up. You don't have to wake me up. I can get up on my own."

Darkly lifted her head off the pillow and squinted. The harsh morning sun flooded in through her hotel room window. She looked above her head at a faded oil painting of a mountain-scape and remembered where she was.

"Damn." She called out to Gus, "Sorry. Be right there."

"No problem. Do you want me to get you some breakfast to eat on the way to set?"

Darkly slapped herself across the face and got out of bed. She pulled on her underwear and a t-shirt. She went to the door and opened it a crack. Gus was sipping a coffee. Darkly reached out and grabbed it out of his hand. She took a long sip.

"Set?"

"You're welcome. Photographer's Assistant, remember?" He whispered. "What are your initial thoughts about this place, anyway? Pretty creepy, huh?"

Darkly grabbed Gus by the shirt and pulled him inside. She kissed him deeply and fumbled with his belt. She reached in to feel he was already hard.

Gus then took control, as she hoped he would, turning her around and slamming her up against the wall, while pulling down her underwear. He entered her, as she reached out and pushed the door shut.

Darkly pulled on her jeans while Gus buttoned up his flannel shirt.

"What do I need to know about photography?"

"Don't worry about it. You can just hold the bag. Give me fresh batteries when I need them."

"Good. Best to keep it simple. Not complicated."

"Right."

Darkly finished dressing and touched up the make-up covering her spider's web of blue veins.

Darkly walked past Lewis to the front door. He was brushing the counter with an old-fashioned feather duster. Darkly was certain he was just moving the dirt around.

"No messages, Miss," he called out.

He looked behind him at a bank of empty hotel mailboxes.

"Oh. Thanks. I probably won't be getting much during my stay. No one from the outside world knows I'm here."

"That's good, Miss."

Creepy is right, Darkly thought, as she and Gus walked out into the sunlight.

Marvin was waiting there in what appeared to be an old army jeep. It was painted with a fresh coat of flat black paint.

"Pretty cool, huh? We rented it off a local farmer. He says it saw action in the Korean War. There are bullet holes! I'd open the doors for you, but there aren't any." Marvin laughed at his own lame joke.

Darkly hopped into the back and looked for the seat-belt.

"Sorry, there aren't any seat belts. It's vintage. Don't worry, I'll take it slow."

Gus hopped into the passenger seat next to Marvin.

"That's a shame, Marv. The lady likes it fast."

Darkly ignored Gus and paid attention to Marvin.

"I'm sure you're a fine driver, Marvin."

Marvin put the jeep into gear and headed down the hill into the water and crossed the ford in the river. The ride was a little bumpy, but with the spray of cold water, Darkly felt a sense of anonymity wash over her. She was alone in the wilderness with people she didn't really know. Not to mention she'd just had sex with someone she didn't really know.

Gus felt the bottom of his jeans get wet. He lifted his camera bag above his head.

"Watch the camera, Marv."

"Yes, sir."

The jeep's transmission complained at climbing the steep hill up to the scenic overlook of the valley and film circus. The sound of metal grinding upon metal was alarming at times, but the engine never seemed in imminent danger of stalling, just exploding.

Darkly looked out over the valley and saw how the Moon River had been given its name. The portion that ran through town copied the shape of a crescent moon.

Darkly could make out the goings-on in the small town. An old man was washing the windows of a storefront, and she saw Sheriff Buck walk into an old stone building with a clock face on the front. That must be the town hall. The clock said it was three fifteen. Broken. This really was a run-down little backwater. By their nature, small places had a monopoly on secrets. It was too early for Darkly to tell if the secrets of Wolf Woods held any consequence.

The town disappeared from sight, as the jeep moved into tree cover and climbed the last quarter mile up to the plateau. Marvin parked the jeep in front of one of the RVs, pulled the hand brake, and popped the clutch into neutral.

"Safe and sound."

"Thank you, Marvin."

Darkly climbed out of the jeep, as Serena poked her head out of the door of her RV.

"Morning." Darkly waved.

Serena smiled at Gus, who smiled back at her.

Darkly felt a twitch of jealousy which she swiftly crushed into the ground.

When the four actors were finally assembled for the first shot on the day's call sheet, Shane was wearing a t-shirt that was tight enough to show off his muscles and white enough to be the perfect canvass for the first murder of the film.

Serena was quite pleased with her costume, too. The denim sleeveless vest chafed her skin a little, but it was flattering in all the right places. She asked Gus if he would help her tape the vest to the bare skin below. He was happy to be of assistance.

Carter was mapping out the shot with his hands for Jake, who stood with a Steadicam strapped to his torso. Gus left Serena satisfied and motioned to Darkly, who was holding a small duffel bag, as he removed the lens off his camera. He handed it to Darkly.

"I need the prime lens."

"And what's that?" she whispered.

"The only other lens in the case."

"Right."

"What I'm handing you is a zoom lens."

"Got it. Tone down the condescension."

"Okay, folks," Carter called for everyone's attention. "Welcome to the first day of filming. Everyone looks the part."

Carter looked out over the distant ridge of hills beyond the Moon River, and the group followed his sight.

"We are on the other side of the hills that separate this valley from the valley of Wolf Woods. The river snakes its way around the base of this hill, through some class two rapids, and then down into town."

Darkly could make out the beginning of the white water only, as the ridge they were on climbed farther and obscured their view into the next valley.

"We'll film you arriving in the jeep later, but today, I want to capture three friends hiking in the woods, discovering the beauty of their surroundings, and drinking from the river. Be creative. Do what comes naturally. Just have fun with it!"

Christopher coughed conspicuously, interrupting Carter's flow.

"Oh, yes, and Christopher's character is watching you the whole time."

"Plotting," Christopher chimed in.

"That's right, plotting and planning. But, the three of you are not aware of this. You haven't spotted him yet. You don't suspect anything, you're completely relaxed. We don't see Chris. The camera is him. His POV. Chris is here on his own accord to get a feel for his character."

"Did someone say method?" Christopher chuckled at his own simple wit.

"Alright. So, Peter and Shane, you two are making your way down the hill towards the river. Serena is holding back a little, taking in the majesty of her surroundings. When you get to the river, remove your packs and take a drink. The water's pure, don't worry. I had some myself."

Darkly stopped counting after the tenth time the actors climbed back up the hill. Every angle was covered while hiking down to the river. She wondered if they were bringing in a helicopter for an aerial view after lunch.

Once lunch did come, Darkly was bursting. She couldn't hold her small bladder for a journey back to the circus, so she speedily slipped away saying she would find her own way back to base camp. Darkly had seen a rock enclosure down alongside the river that would provide the perfect amount of privacy.

She ran uncomfortably along the riverbank until reaching the group of rocks that jutted out into the bend in the river. It was at this bend that the water picked up speed, careening into a rock face, and then abruptly changing direction.

Darkly climbed up onto a boulder deposited some time during the last ice age and looked down onto a whirlpool of swirling white foam. A piece of driftwood was caught in a boomerang effect, threatening to beach itself like the other river debris that littered the pebbles at the edge of the water, before being sucked back into the vortex.

Darkly peered down the side of the boulder she hadn't climbed. The giant rock masked a hole in the hillside that was boarded up with plywood. Darkly slid onto her stomach and groaned. This was getting painful. Her toes found indentations in the rock face, and she climbed back down to earth, jumping the last couple feet.

She couldn't wait any longer. She fumbled with her buttons and stepped out of her jeans. She leaned against the rock and watched the water by her side rush by on its way into town.

To her right, she could see that the plywood covering the hole in the hillside was rotting away from the constant spray of the rapids. Gaping holes could easily allow a person to crawl inside. A tin sign hung off one of the wooden planks by a rusty nail. It proclaimed the word "DANGER" in flaking red paint.

Darkly finished her business and fastened the belt around her waist once again. Rather than climb back up the boulder to the ridge, she decided she would take a longer, but gentler route that took her along the bend in the river. After this section, she could hike back up the hill through a meadow of wild flowers below the circus of film trailers.

But what was this hole? Darkly had heard about the gold rush out West. Was this an actual mine from the 19th Century? No doubt Carter would think it an excellent place for the friends to hide from Christopher's serial killer character. She decided she'd poke her head inside and see if there was actually any room for a camera. It looked pretty dark from here. By now, it was probably a jumble of caved in timbers and dirt.

Darkly rummaged around inside Gus's camera case. The Boy Scout came prepared. She pulled out a flashlight.

The boards were soft from years of exposure to the elements, and Darkly had no problem making one of the holes even bigger by breaking pieces off and throwing them into the water to be eaten by the whirlpool.

She shone the flashlight inside and was surprised to see empty space ahead. There was no overturned mine cart buried under a mountain of immovable rock. Darkly waved the beam of light to either side of the interior. She found walls and a ceiling sculpted into the hill. This was an intact tunnel.

She pointed the flashlight directly ahead. The tunnel must go on for some distance, as the light didn't touch a back wall. Then she saw it: a glint in the wall. Actually, it was a sparkle. Several of them. Sparkles. More than several. There were stars in the walls of the tunnel. They couldn't be diamonds, surely. It wouldn't have been abandoned and boarded up if the hill was full of diamonds. Darkly had to know what that sparkle was.

Her father always told her she was the most curious creature he had ever known. "Curiosity killed the cat, so better you have the nose of a dog." But, Darkly could never abide a mystery.

So, she crawled on all fours into an abandoned shaft that was designated dangerous and which could collapse on her head at any second and bury her forever, entombed in the remote wilderness.

She found the tunnel was high enough that she could fully stand up on the other side of the wooden barrier. She reached up with her hand and felt the rough ceiling of the tunnel about six inches above her head. It was stone that showered particles of dust and dirt onto her face when she rubbed it. Darkly coughed and shook her hair clean.

She shone the flashlight on the ground ahead. She couldn't make out any obstructions. She slid her feet along the dirt floor until she felt certain it was perfectly solid and that she wasn't going to fall through to a lower level that descended all the way to Hell for all she knew.

Darkly approached one of the walls and walked forward. Her hand kept contact with the surface, and her flashlight focused on the reflection of starlight ahead.

Darkly's hand was now feeling only air, and she turned her beam of light down another tunnel that branched off the entrance chamber. A light, cool breeze tickled her cheek. The stars shone brighter just a few paces ahead. The tunnel widened out into the semblance of a room. Darkly felt her calf muscles tighten as the gradient became steep. She was walking downhill, deeper underground.

Darkly brushed her light across the face of the surrounding rock, and the walls erupted in color. Veins of purple and blue coated the surface. Darkly reached out and ran her fingers over the jagged edges of a quarry of quartz crystal. It extended into a dome over her head. She had the sensation of being in a planetarium or inside a massive version of the geode her high school science teacher had kept on his desk.

"Holy Mother of God."

Darkly was not easily impressed. She stepped forward, following the veins farther underground and went crashing to her knees. She hadn't noticed the small ledge as the ground gave way twelve inches beneath her into a lower level of the room. Darkly braced her fall with the flashlight, and her only source of light, aside from the faint shards of sunlight extending from the entrance, was extinguished.

Gus did not question why Darkly did not join him for lunch. They were on an investigation after all. She could take care of herself. Although it would be appropriate procedure to let him know of her whereabouts, it was not mandatory. She was the senior officer. Besides, his assistance was required again by one of the actors. Having seen him in action with Serena, Shane had asked Gus to his trailer to assist him with what he described as a wardrobe malfunction. Great. He was a decorated Mountie turned set bitch. Wasn't this Marvin's job?

Darkly was startled, but uninjured. She still had the flashlight in her hand. She slapped it and shook it. Nothing. The bulb must have broken.

"Don't panic, Darkly. Even a baby could crawl back outside."

Then, Darkly remembered Victoria's lighter. Well, technically it was the lighter that Victoria stole off Christopher. She felt the outline of the small butane lighter through her back pocket. She pulled it out with her fingertips, held it close to her face and lit it. She looked down at her elbows. They were a little bruised, but no blood.

Darkly waved the flame in front of the ledge. It was really just a small step. She turned her attention to the stone floor. A few inches from her feet, smiling back at her, was a human skull. Darkly gasped and leapt back, slamming her back into the step and letting go of the top of the lighter which extinguished the flame.

"Christ!"

Darkly sat there in the dark for a minute and took a deep breath before relighting the flame. She held her hand out into the black void. Next to the skull lay a pile of leg and arm bones. Beyond those, another skull and another. The floor was littered with skeletons.

Wait a minute! Were these fake? Had Carter's team placed these here?

"That's all it is," Darkly deduced.

This was Christopher's serial killer lair. Oh, no. She'd destroyed the set when tearing away the boards.

Darkly reached out and picked up the skull. The lower jaw fell off and broke in two on the ground. There we go, something else she'd have to pay for. Darkly examined the skull up close. Was it porcelain? Clay? It felt like real bone. She picked out grooves on the top of the head. They looked like knife cuts. She turned the skull upside down. The cavity was full of dirt. She shook it out and examined the upper jaw. Two of the molars were capped with crowns. This thing was real.

Darkly dropped it and backed up, propping herself onto the ledge. She was getting the hell out of here.

Then, Darkly heard it: a low, guttural growl. Then, she saw them. Her flame reflected off two yellow pin pricks floating in the darkness. The eyes were moving towards her.

Darkly swung her feet up onto the ledge, as a big, shaggy, black and white dog came into view. It was holding a femur bone in its mouth, bearing its teeth at Darkly. Darkly knew better than to run. If she ran, she was meat with the potential for bone. She needed to placate the animal.

Darkly rolled a skull towards the dog.

"I don't want the bones, boy. They're all yours," she said in her calmest, sweetest voice.

"Milly!"

The voice echoed through the tunnel.

"Milly! Come on, girl!"

The dog turned its head to the direction of the tunnel entrance, whimpered, and leapt past Darkly, racing towards the voice it clearly knew and loved.

"Hello?!" Darkly called out.

"Hello? Who's there? You alright?" It was a young man's voice.

"Uh, I'm on the film shoot. I, uh, my flashlight broke."

"Okay. I'll be right there."

Darkly could hear someone sliding along the dirt by the entrance, pulling wooden boards aside, then shuffling in her direction. A flashlight beam illuminated the tunnel and made its way along the floor to Darkly's position. The light leapt up into the air, fixing on an attractive teenage boy's face and black wavy hair that swept down over his forehead.

"Hi. I'm Trey. Need some help?"

Milly brushed past Trey, walked up to Darkly, and licked her face.

"Oh, now you want to be friends," Darkly said and grabbed hold of the dog's silky soft ears.

CHAPTER NINE

Buck hammered the last of the planks over the mine's entrance and put the warning sign back in place. Milly crouched down and shoved her nose under one of the planks and cried.

"Trey. Get her out of here, would ya."

"Come on, girl. I'll find you a bone at home."

Buck's son looked over at Darkly.

"A chicken bone."

He then slipped his fingers under Milly's collar and pulled her away from the tunnel. "Go on!" He let loose of Milly, and the dog ran with abandon along the riverside, barking at and chasing the driftwood being carried downriver by the rapids. Trey ran after her.

"Thanks again, Trey!"

The seventeen-year-old turned and smiled at Darkly, before disappearing around the bend in the river.

Carter, Marvin, and the cast leaned against the rocks around the mine entrance, waiting for the sheriff to give them the okay to resume filming.

"Are you sure I couldn't persuade you to let us use it? Just for an afternoon?"

Carter was chomping at the bit to get into the mine. This was exactly what his movie needed. But, Buck wasn't budging.

"I got enough to deal with without having every chief in the region breathing down my neck. They're sensitive about their ancient burial places."

"Sheriff, how ancient can the mine be? I mean, the gold rush was in the mid-1800s, wasn't it?" Darkly asked.

Darkly wasn't buying the sheriff's story.

"One of the early settlers from the town discovered the cave and the quartz chamber. Where there's quartz, there's often gold," Buck explained. "The town buried the Indian bodies they found entombed in there and proceeded to carve out more tunnels under ground. Never found much of anything. There was more gold in the river."

"So, where did these bodies come from, Sheriff?" Carter asked.

Carter was intrigued. How could he fit this into his story?

"In the early twentieth century, the town made amends with the local tribes, dug up the bodies, and restored them to their rightful resting place. Those skeletons are hundreds of years old."

Buck slid his hammer into his tool belt and turned to go.

"Now if you'll excuse me, I have work to do."

He walked up to Darkly.

"I'm sorry you had a scare. Next time, pay attention to the sign. It was there for a reason. Miss."

Buck nodded at Darkly and walked past her to follow the path his son had taken back to town. Darkly found she liked being told off by Sheriff Buck. She watched him walk off and noticed Christopher slip away from the group to say something to Buck from a discreet distance.

Buck did not look pleased to listen to anything Christopher had to say. He merely shook his head once and continued on his way.

Carter snapped Darkly out of her trance.

"Well, people, Darkly's okay, and we have to respect the religious rites of the indigenous population. Let's get back to work."

The cast and crew clambered over the large rocks by the riverside and began the trek back up the hill. Darkly was the last to climb up, accepting Marvin's hand. As he pulled her up, a thought struck her. The skeletons were hundreds of years old. Why did the skull she handled have shiny, silver crowns over the teeth? What did the ancient first nation's people know about dentistry?

Darkly and Gus were beat by the time Marvin dropped them outside the hotel. The bumpy ride home hadn't stopped her from dozing. Upon entering the hotel, Darkly found Lewis concentrating on an mp3 player; he turned it over and examined it end to end, adjusting the earbuds clamped to the side of his head. Darkly decided to have some fun.

"Any messages for me?"

Lewis looked back at the empty wooden box that represented Darkly's room.

"Nope."

"You need some help with that?"

Lewis's eyes brightened. "I can't turn it on."

Darkly reached out her hand. Lewis pulled the player close to his body like a child protecting his peanut butter and jelly sandwich from a bully.

"It was a gift."

"If the battery's run down, you're going to need to plug it into a USB cord to recharge it."

From Lewis's expression, Darkly might as well have been speaking in Chinese.

"It comes with a cord that connects the player to your computer, and the computer recharges the player."

"But I don't have a Com Puter."

"Strange gift for someone who doesn't have a computer." Darkly resisted the urge to imitate Lewis's pronunciation of the word.

Lewis removed the earbuds from his hairy ears and placed the mp3 player in a drawer under the check-in counter. He glared at Darkly. She had clearly burst his balloon.

"As I said, there are no messages for you."

Lewis left Darkly standing in front of the desk and disappeared behind a door with the word "Management" etched into the wood.

Darkly woke up to the sound of her stomach rumbling. The room was pitch black. She had only meant to take a nap, but the day had sapped her energy. She'd slept right through supper.

Darkly lay there, listening, trying to determine if any of the movie's cast were in their rooms. She could make out a faint sound. It was music. An organ, she thought. That was weird.

Her stomach rumbled again. She'd better eat something or she'd be a wreck tomorrow. Darkly groped for the bedside lamp and turned it on. She picked up her useless cellphone. Well, it wasn't completely useless when plugged in. It was her watch, alarm clock, and note taker, as well. It was just a few minutes past nine. Maybe the diner was still open? Or at least some corner shop? She'd kill for a falafel sandwich or a kebab right now, but she'd settle for a bag of salt and vinegar chips and a diet coke.

Darkly threw on a pair of jeans and a sweat shirt, and she tiptoed out into the hallway. She could hear laughing coming from the room a couple doors down. It sounded like Shane, Serena and Peter. She was pretty sure she could smell pot. Partaking would only make her more hungry and cause her to fail the next mandated drug test, so she walked right on by. Christopher had taped a headshot to his front door and a manila envelope below it for rewrites. Loud snoring drifted out from within.

Darkly thought about knocking on Gus's door. But, she was back in that mode of thinking that she didn't need him, and she didn't want to make him think she needed him. She was just going out for a stroll.

Darkly made her way down to the deserted lobby and out the door into a cool, breezy night. She decided to walk in the direction of the music, which was easily identifiable now as a church organ accompanied by an out of tune but pious chorus.

The night sky was cloudy. Darkly used the church windows as a beacon as she made her way down the main street of closed shops and abandoned buildings. Despite the lack of light, Darkly could make out chained doors and broken windowpanes. She knew the economy was bad, but she wondered how anyone could afford to live in this town. There had to be some sort of barter system in place.

Darkly finally found what she was looking for: Barry's Cash and Carry. There was a lone light on in the shop. She walked up to the door and tried the handle. Of course it was locked. From the sound of the choir, Barry was probably in church with the rest of the town. Praying for a new life in a better location?

Darkly noticed the sign in the window informing her of the hours of operation. Ten in the morning until noon, and then, two until four p.m., Monday through Saturday. Except Wednesday, when Barry closed for the day at noon. Printed below the hours, the sign read, "Trespassers will be punished."

Darkly's stomach was rumbling at this point, and she fantasized whether one more broken window would make a difference in this place.

Just to torture herself, Darkly leaned her forehead against the glass and searched for her salt and vinegar chips. The cashier's counter had an old analog register and a jar of pickled eggs next to it. Behind the register, there was a rack of cigarettes, about a dozen in total.

"Must not be many smokers. At least, they're healthy rednecks," Darkly mused.

The magazine rack next to the counter was completely empty. In place of the magazines, there were little notecards and sheets of paper taped to the rack. They advertised things like chainsaw for sale, piano lessons, and other innocuous rural listings.

One note did seem strange to Darkly. "WAX JOB. NO HAIR FOR TWO CYCLES. TALK TO BETH." Waxing?

The rest of the store looked like a Soviet food bank: a box of crackers here, a can of soup there, two apples in a basket, and some jars of preserves and pickled vegetables with homemade labels. Darkly gave up. She was going hungry tonight. Unless, she thought, the church is throwing a potluck. She'd more than pay for her supper with tales of life in the big city.

She crossed the street and climbed stone steps to the double oak doors of the church entrance. This time, she found a door that was unlocked, and she slipped inside. The foyer contained a couple benches and community bulletin boards with notices of upcoming church events.

The wall that separated the foyer from the sanctuary was made up of wood panels from the floor to waste height. Above that, the wall gave way to panels of stained glass. Darkly could make out the silhouettes of parishioners through the glass.

The stained glass panels displayed what Darkly assumed was a biblical story. In the first panel, a man in flowing robes of purple wearing a golden crown stood before a city with an army behind him. Rays of sunlight shone down on the city, but storm clouds darkened the sky above the king.

In the second panel, the king walked among the dead of the city. His soldiers stood over crying women and children, impaling them with their swords. This gave way to the third panel, in which the king bowed before an angel with his hands clasped together in a pleading prayer. The angel held the king's crown in his hand and pointed at a forest behind the king.

Darkly studied the final panel. The great king now scrounged on the ground for acorns. His hair was matted; his teeth were like fangs. His nails had grown sharp as claws, and hair covered his body instead of clothes.

"Clearly a very bad man," Darkly whispered to herself.

The singing of a hymn stopped, and Darkly heard the congregation sit in unison. A door in between panel two and three led to the sanctuary. Darkly stepped close to it and positioned her eye over the crack in the door. She could make out a few heads in her line of vision and had a good view of the altar where the preacher stood. He wore the traditional black, with a white collar that had turned the same shade of yellow as the stained mane of white hair that covered his head. His frame was bent, but his eyes were not tired. They were alert and searched the faces of his parishioners for anticipation of what he was about to say.

He took an audible breath in and spoke. His voice was raspy, but carried the weight of years of authority.

"There are those among us who struggle with faith. In fact, I myself have wrestled with that demon who goes by the name of Doubt. Yes, it is true. That might comfort some of you and worry others."

The preacher smiled and took a sip of water.

"Worry, regret, fear, all of these are temporary lapses in our faith in God's plan. Upon your journeys home tonight, I ask you to reflect on why it is we gather here on Wednesday nights to raise our voices in song. It is not some Oriental chant to empty our minds. It is an act of praise and a reminder to us all that even the basest among us are worthy of forgiveness. Never forget the dread king. He was punished by God for his pride and for his sins committed against the Lord's chosen people. But, in seven years, he was forgiven and restored to his former status."

The preacher paused and stared into the eyes of one of the parishioners whose head Darkly could only see from behind.

The preacher repeated his last words, "To his former status, my friends. Think of the opportunity that presents itself to our community. Such a gift from God. If only we may prove ourselves worthy of it."

With these words, Buck stood and left his pew. He was headed in Darkly's direction.

"Humility in the face of God," the preacher called after Buck. "We must show him our worth in our actions."

Buck put his sheriff's hat on inside the church.

This was no potluck. Darkly turned to make a hasty exit and ran right into the largest barrel chest she had ever encountered. She looked up at the face of a man with small, squinting eyes. His hair was long and oily, and his beard much the same. He was dressed in a lumberjack's shirt, overalls, and dirty boots. He held a wooden box in his hand. The box lid dangled from a rusty hinge.

"Here to steal from us all? Here to take from those who have nothing?"

The giant man leaned into Darkly, as the door to the sanctuary swung open behind her. Buck almost ran into them both.

"What the hell? Ed, what's going on here?"

Ed held the empty box up for Buck to see.

"She stole the tithes, Sheriff. Outsiders are no good. Should have done something the moment they got here."

"Ed, put the damn box back where it belongs. There hasn't been so much as a nickel dropped in that thing for the past nine months."

Ed just stood there, scowling at Darkly.

"Ed, put it back."

Ed begrudgingly placed the tithe box back where it belonged and slammed the lid shut, breaking the rusty hinge in the process.

Buck shook his head. "Don't you think you should be keeping an eye on your sheep, Ed? You lose the most at night when no one's watching, don't you? If you like, I'll send my boy over so that you and your daughter can both get some sleep at the same time."

Ed turned his attention to Buck, and the two locked each other in their sights for a few interminable seconds.

"Your ear's healed nicely, Ed."

Ed nodded his head and instinctually reached up to touch his perfectly-formed ear.

"I've said my peace. Anything more would be inappropriate in a house of God. Tell your boy to bring Milly. There's work for a dog now, too."

Ed turned and left.

Darkly started breathing again.

"I was hungry. I thought it might be a church social, you know?"

"Moonshine and square dancing was last week."

Buck wasn't a natural at humor, but there was something about Darkly that inspired him to make an effort.

CHAPTER TEN

It had been a surprisingly good meal. A free-range omelet with honey-cured ham and fresh berries from the surrounding woods. Even Buck's wine was good. It was no Napa Valley vintage, but Darkly did not find it difficult to polish off half a bottle.

Buck had changed out of his uniform into a pair of jeans and a plain white t-shirt. He appeared as care-free as she suspected he was capable. With the full head of hair that fell down over his ears, he reminded her of a California surfer boy. He also had the longest eyelashes Darkly had ever seen on a man.

"You seem to like my wine," Buck said, as he topped up Darkly's glass.

"It's the finest cherry wine I've ever had."

She giggled. She was definitely feeling the effects of the alcohol.

"Elderberry," Buck corrected her.

"Well, in fact, it's the only elderberry wine to have ever passed beyond these lips."

She pointed haphazardly at her lips.

"We don't get a lot of supplies from the outside world. We're off the beaten path up here. We grow and make most of what we need."

"Sounds idyllic."

"It can be. Like any lifestyle, it has its appeal and its limitations."

Buck cleared the empty plates off the kitchen table and filled the sink with water. His house was a log cabin on the edge of town. It was comfortable and clean. The fixtures were a few models previous, but were all in working order. There was no TV, but there was a stereo and a guitar propped up in one corner of the living room. A couple of bedrooms and a full bath completed the house.

Darkly joined Buck at the sink.

"I'm a good drier."

Buck tossed her a towel. Darkly dashed back to the table and grabbed the glasses of wine.

"My grandmother always told me that when you open a bottle of wine, you finish it."

"Your grandmother sounds like a wise woman."

Buck poured most of his glass into Darkly's.

"But, as for me, I'm always on duty."

Buck passed Darkly a plate, and she wiped it dry.

"Tell me, Buck, how does—I mean, your name doesn't really suit you." Darkly put her hand on Buck's arm. "I'm sorry. I'm not trying to hurt your feelings or anything."

Buck shrugged it off. "No offense taken. It was better than the alternative. My parents named me Buckwald."

"You could have changed your name altogether."

Darkly removed her hand after leaving it on his arm a tad longer than was wise between strangers.

Buck moved a little closer to Darkly.

"I don't know what it's like where you're from, but here, changing your name is like disowning your family."

"I see."

This close, Darkly could smell Buck. He smelled clean. She hoped she smelled the same to him. Buck continued to wash, and Darkly dried. Neither spoke. It was quiet. It was nice. At one point, Buck reached his hand up to scratch his neck. She watched the water left behind trickle down his skin. It made Darkly begin to perspire.

Right then, there was a sudden banging on Buck's front door. Did Darkly hear Buck right? Did Buck just growl? Buck stepped back and dried his hands.

"Excuse me."

Darkly smiled consolingly. "Always on duty." She finished off her wine.

Buck opened the door, and Geraldine came bursting in like water through a broken levy.

"There's been—" She saw Darkly and stopped.

Darkly recognized the split-second look of pure venom in Geraldine's eyes. Geraldine quickly recovered and ran to Darkly with open arms.

"Oh, sweetheart, I'm so sorry. There's been a terrible accident. One of your friends is dead, darling."

Doc Ross stood over Christopher's mutilated body next to the dumpster in the alley behind the hotel. He snapped a couple photos with an old Kodak camera.

The actor's clothes had been torn off and chunks of flesh ripped clean from his ribs. Doc covered the body with a sheet and turned to Buck.

"I'll get these developed. There's nothing else I can do." He glanced at Geraldine. "This thing is no longer just a nuisance."

Doc walked off down the alleyway to where Carter, Gus, Marvin, Jake, and the cast stood waiting.

"I'll need to arrange transport to his next of kin," he explained. The inquest will be speedy. Not much nuance to a bear mauling.

I'm truly sorry for your loss. Come see me in the morning, if you need anything."

Doc shook his head and left.

Buck knelt down by Christopher's body and studied the ground for a moment, concentrating.

Darkly broke the silence. "I heard him snoring, sound asleep when I left the hotel."

"You were lucky, darling," Geraldine responded. "This could have been you. He must have come out the back exit of the hotel and surprised the bear. The bear only did what comes naturally. Isn't that right, Buck?"

Darkly could have sworn on a Bible that Geraldine was coaching Buck.

"Geraldine, I'm gonna need your walk-in freezer to store the body until we can figure out what the next of kin want to do. I'm going to need Trey's help in moving it."

"Are you going to track it down and kill it?"

Darkly asked the question to see what Geraldine's reaction would be. She hadn't worked out yet the reason behind her own curiosity.

Buck stood up into the full authority of his position.

"As Geraldine said, it was only doing what comes naturally."

"That's right. It had nothing against Sam. He was competition for the meal in that dumpster."

"His name was Christopher, Gerri," Buck said, correcting Geraldine.

"Sorry. Christopher. Yes. Poor man."

"But doesn't it have a taste for human flesh now? It will come back," Serena said with the conviction of a bear expert.

She was constantly looking around her, anticipating the famished beast's return.

"If it does, we'll deal with it then." Buck found Carter with his gaze. "I expect you'll be wanting to pack up and leave. Find a safer location."

"No," Geraldine interjected, "Their friend wouldn't want that, Buck. Christopher wouldn't want that. The show must go on, isn't that what they say?"

"Lewis keeps a bottle of single malt under the front desk. I'm sure you all could use a drink."

This was Buck's way of dismissing the cast and crew.

Carter was in shock. Every step forward in his life had been followed by a few steps back. This time, he'd been knocked off his feet. But, he figured he had to say something helpful.

"The sheriff says we should all go inside. The bear could still be around. Let's get some sleep."

Darkly walked past the open mouths. They all turned and followed her into the hotel.

Geraldine lowered her voice. "We begin early. Before they finish the movie. That's all this means. No one would ever see it anyway."

Buck walked up to the hotel's back exit and examined the door. He took out a handkerchief from his back pocket and wiped the handle. He looked down at the blood that now dyed the white square red. Surprisingly, Buck continued to wipe the handle spotlessly clean.

"Looks like she toyed with him."

Buck folded the handkerchief neatly and put it in his pocket.

"This wasn't how things were supposed to go. Get your walk-in ready, Geraldine."

"If you come for her, you'll have to answer to your son."

"They haven't mated yet."

"Are you sure about that, Buck?"

CHAPTER ELEVEN

Victoria topped up Darkly's coffee cup and took her order of scrambled eggs and coffee. As she took her first sip, there it was. The coffee's bitter flavor was overtaken by the taste of death. Darkly looked into Victoria's eyes. The girl was a million miles away. Then, strangely, the coffee's natural flavor recovered, and death seemed to Darkly to be banished from Victoria once again.

Across the table, Carter appeared at the end of his rope. The director had confined his responses to a tilt of the head up until this point. He was also a little worse for wear after consuming half a bottle of whisky the sheriff had so kindly pointed him in the direction of.

"Well, I'm going to say it." It was Shane who broke the silence. "I know we aren't supposed to speak negatively about the dead, but Christopher rubbed me the wrong way right from the start."

"Oh, Shane."

Serena was growing more nauseous by the minute. She opened her container of silver supplements and popped the cure-all into her mouth.

Peter then asked the question they all were thinking. "Can't we just continue filming without him? I mean, most of the shots are from his POV, aren't they? He's really just a shadow in the woods. We don't even see his face until the final stand-off."

"And when it comes time to see his face?" Shane asked.

Marvin was already thinking about a casting session among the locals.

Outside, Trey was standing with Millie, beckoning to Victoria to join him. Victoria ran out the door into Trey's arms. He stroked her hair and kissed her.

"We cast a local. We make an event out of the auditions. They get to go to the premiere, and Carter talks about a local talent discovery with the press. Maybe we even do a screening in the town. You know, we spruce up the local movie theater. We buy them a new popcorn machine or something." Marvin's words captured Carter's attention.

"It could work."

Carter had opened his mouth for the first time that morning and even took a bite of his breakfast.

"I'm in," said Peter.

Christopher's gruesome death hadn't ruined his appetite. Peter was ready for a second helping of breakfast.

Shane wasn't far behind.

"I feel bad about what happened, but I need the money. You ready to go back to waiting tables already, S?"

Serena shook her head in response to Shane, while Darkly was distracted by the lovebirds outside. She watched them split apart when Buck pulled up across the street, got out of his pickup truck, and walked up to his son. Trey took a protective position in front of Victoria. Buck shook his head and walked into the diner.

Gus nudged Darkly and whispered, "Hey, voyeur, something interesting?"

The cowbell over the diner door clanked. Buck removed his hat and walked right up to the cast and crew table.

Marvin leapt up and offered Buck his seat.

"I've finished eating, Sheriff. You can have my chair."

"Have a seat, son. I've eaten already."

Buck placed his hand on the back of Darkly's chair, but said what he came to say to Carter.

"The inquest over your actor's death will take place tonight, if you would like to attend."

"We'll all be there, Sheriff," Marvin answered for Carter.

"Is there any question as to how Christopher died?" Darkly asked.

"An inquest is a legal formality. It will only take about twenty minutes. The person who found him is questioned by the magistrate, the cause of death made official, and you folks can go home."

Carter regained command. "And what if we wanted to stay and finish the movie, Sheriff?"

Buck didn't respond right away. But when he did, Darkly thought he sounded relieved.

"The town would prefer for you to stay and complete your work, of course."

"Good." Carter looked out among his cast. "I think we're decided."

Then, as an afterthought that revealed exactly where Carter's priorities were, he asked, "And what about the body?"

"I'm afraid that unless you can arrange that transport in the next forty-eight hours, we'll have to bury the body. I can't keep him here in the diner walk-in any longer than that without breaking the town's health code. As the enforcer of that code, I have no such intention of abusing it."

Serena looked at the fork in her hand. Scrambled eggs spilled off, and she dropped the utensil.

"He's here? Where you keep the food?" she asked Buck.

"He's sealed in a body bag, ma'am. Perfectly safe. We're too small a town to have a morgue. During the winter, we keep the dead in the church basement until the ground softens in the spring."

Buck put his hat back on.

"The inquest will be at the church at seven tonight. Don't be surprised if a few of the locals show up to watch. These things are a social event on a calendar packed with very little to do."

Buck walked past Victoria, who had returned to her work and was wiping down the diner counter. Neither acknowledged each other.

Darkly picked up a piece of toast off Serena's plate and took a bite.

"Finished?"

Serena glared at Darkly.

"They don't keep the toast in the fridge."

Bread was one of the few things Serena could stomach in this place.

The inquest was held in the church. A large arm chair and a wooden desk had been set up below the altar. Reverend MacIntyre held the position of magistrate in addition to his divine duties, and clearly relished the few opportunities he had to practice secular law. He wore a flowing, if threadbare, black robe, and a matted, discolored wig piece was perched precariously on the crown of his head.

Everyone from the film's cast and crew was seated just below MacIntyre. Behind them, the entire town had congregated. Geraldine, Lewis, Ed, and Buck sat behind Darkly's pew. There was even a gathering of teens at the back of the church. Victoria and Trey were pressed closely together at the end of the last pew. Darkly wore black. It's true she usually wore black, but this time it was out of respect.

MacIntyre rapped his gavel on the desk.

"I call this session to order. The inquest into the death of Christopher Spalding will now take place. I would like to commend you all on your interest in our town's civic affairs. I hope to see all of you again this Sunday."

Macintyre smiled, proud of his little jab. He chuckled a little, cleared his throat, rapped the gavel once, and despite knowing where Buck was seated, looked over and past him into the general direction of the pews.

"Will the law enforcement officer responsible for this case please take the stand?"

As far as Darkly knew, Buck was the only law enforcement officer in this town.

Buck stood up and approached the pulpit. He took his position behind the lectern as though he was going to read a psalm from the giant, gold-enameled Bible that was placed on top of it. He placed his hand on the Bible.

"Please state your name for the court, Sheriff."

"Buckwald Robertson. I am sheriff of Wolf Woods."

"Thank you, Sheriff. And do you attest to the truth and accuracy of what you are about to say?"

"I do."

Buck removed his hand from the Bible, and Macintyre looked down at the paper in front of him.

"Sheriff, when you were called to the scene, was the victim already deceased?"

"Yes, Magistrate."

"And what in your professional opinion was the cause of death?"

"Bear mauling. Everything I saw was consistent with that."

"And you have witnessed such a mauling before?"

"Four or five times. Not during. After the fact."

"Of course. Thank you, Sheriff. Before you step down, would you tell us who discovered the body?"

"Mr. Carter Abel."

"And is he present in this court?"

"Yes, he is."

"That is all. You may step down, Sheriff."

Buck returned to his seat next to Geraldine.

"The court now calls Mr. Carter Abel to the stand."

Carter got up from his seat next to Darkly and squeezed past Serena, Peter, and Shane to make his way to the pulpit.

"Please place your hand on the Holy Bible, Mr. Carter, and state your name."

Carter cleared his throat. "Yes, of course."

His voice cracked a little. He was nervous. No doubt still shaken up, Darkly thought. A sensitive guy.

"My name is Carter William Abel."

"Mr. Carter, do you attest to the truth and accuracy of what you are about to say?"

"I do."

Carter kept his hand fixed on the Bible. Had it become a crutch, Darkly wondered?

"You may remove your hand now, Mr. Carter."

"Oh, of course."

Carter slid his hand into his pocket.

"Do you know what time it was when you discovered Mr. Spalding's body, Mr. Carter?"

"It was around ten-thirty."

"I know last night was disturbing, Mr. Carter, but would you take us through the evening?"

"I'm sorry?"

"What you were doing up until you found the body and then afterwards until the sheriff arrived?"

"Oh, right. I, uh, was in my room at the hotel."

"The Royal Inn?" Macintyre prodded. "It's a formality, but we must be precise with the facts."

"Yes, sir. I was in my room. I had finished some re-writes on the scenes for the next day, uh, today. I felt like having a cigarette. You can smoke in the hotel, but I've gotten used to stepping outside to smoke. Everyone does in Miami and L.A. I left my room and walked out of the hotel."

"Alone?"

"Yes, alone."

Macintyre made a quick note on a pad of paper in front of him.

"I like to walk when I smoke, so I decided to walk around the hotel. When I made it to the back of the hotel, I found Christopher lying by the dumpster. He wasn't moving."

"Did you check for a pulse, Mr. Carter?"

"No, I didn't. I'm not even sure I would know how to do that. I ran back into the hotel."

"And you contacted the sheriff then?"

"Uh, no. I tried to wake-up the hotel owner, but he didn't answer the bell. I had Geraldine's phone number on me, so I called her. She told me she would go get the sheriff."

"And then what did you do?"

"I woke up my cast and crew, and we waited in the hotel lobby for the sheriff to show up."

"Are they all present here?"

"Yes. Well, except Jake. He's guarding the equipment at our base camp."

"Guarding? Are you worried someone from this community will rob you?"

"No, sir. Although my music player has gone missing."

"Your what? Record player?"

"Nothing. Never mind."

"And did the sheriff come alone last night?"

"No. He brought with him Geraldine, Doctor Ross, and Darkly Stewart. She had been at the sheriff's house, I believe."

MacIntyre looked over at Darkly.

"Had she?"

His eyes narrowed slightly, then he returned his gaze to Carter.

"Thank you, Mr. Carter. The court has been advised by Doctor Ross that the fatal injuries sustained by Mr. Spalding were consistent with those inflicted by a bear. He has signed a sworn affidavit to that effect."

MacIntyre held a piece of paper up for those in the pews to see.

"Doc is unable to attend these proceedings, as he is attending to an illness."

MacIntyre made a couple more notes before saying, "And Mr. Carter, I have been informed by the sheriff that you are to handle the transport of Mr. Spalding back to his next of kin?"

"Yes, sir. The sheriff allowed my locations manager to use his landline, but he was unable to locate any next-of-kin."

"None at all?"

"No, sir. I didn't know him well really."

"Then I have no choice but to order the burial of Mr. Spalding in the town's cemetery, in accordance with town statutes."

MacIntyre rapped his gavel on the desk.

"Make it so. Mr. Carter, I thank you for your testimony."

"It's Mr. Abel."

"I beg your pardon?"

MacIntyre was confused. He hadn't asked a question.

"You keep calling me Mr. Carter. It's Abel. My last name is Abel."

MacIntyre sat back in his chair and adopted a contrite manner.

"I am terribly sorry, Mr. Abel." MacIntyre carefully spoke the last name to give it its due. "No offense was intended. I was reading about U.S. President Carter the other day. A good Christian, tolerant man. His name must have stuck in my head."

Carter nodded his own head, satisfied with the explanation.

"I was a fan too."

"Oh my, he's not dead, is he?" MacIntyre became immediately and genuinely saddened.

"No, sorry, I meant, you know, he hasn't been the president for over thirty years."

MacIntyre became more confused. "He isn't the president of the United States any longer?"

Darkly couldn't believe it. This town on the edge of nowhere had put its soul and the wheels of justice in the hands of a man who was losing his mind.

Buck cleared his throat loudly, and MacIntyre looked out at the sheriff. The old vicar patted his forehead with a handkerchief and stared momentarily at his gavel with great concentration. He tentatively hit the table with the small mallet, which sparked a renewed comprehension of what the hell he was doing sitting there.

"It is the determination of this court of inquest that the cause of death of Mr. Spalding was bear attack. The crown offers its condolences to the victim's family, should they ever be located. You may now step down, Mr. Car--Mr. Abel."

"Thank you."

Carter moved in front of the pulpit, stopped, and looked back at the magistrate.

MacIntyre looked up from his paperwork.

"You may return to your seat, Mr. Abel."

"No, uh, sir, there's something else."

MacIntyre removed his spectacles.

"Yes, Mr. Abel?"

"When I found Chris, I'm not sure, but I think I may have seen something running away."

"Ah. You saw the bear, Mr. Abel. Fascinating creatures, are they not?"

Darkly almost laughed out loud at the impropriety of the remark.

"Actually, I thought it was a girl. A naked girl."

CHAPTER TWELVE

Buck needed none of his skills to follow the tracks. It had rained the night before, and the trail was muddy. Clumps of yellowish clay stuck to the bottoms of his boots, giving Buck a couple more inches in height every fifty yards or so. He stopped to scrape the mucky growth off onto tree bark.

It was the ears he saw first. They flew out of the brush. Tufts of chestnut brown hair pointing straight and alert had detected his approach and now turned the tables on the hunter.

Buck didn't have a chance. He reached for the strap of the rifle hanging over his shoulder anyway and was on the ground a split second later, staring into the yellow eyes of the wolf whose teeth were snapping the bone of his forearm in two.

Buck knew he had seconds before he would succumb to panic and shock. He reached for the knife in his belt, slashed up into the wolf's throat, and sliced through the jugular.

The wolf yelped and let go of Buck's arm. It staggered back, shaking its head as though trying to rid itself of pestering gnats.

Blood splayed across Buck's face, and the wolf shook itself into death. As he turned away from the gruesome scene, Buck quickly learned the wolf was not alone. A black wolf raced down the trail, barreling down on Buck, bent on avenging its mate.

Buck reached for his rifle once again, propped it up between his legs and shifted the weapon's bolt into place. With one hand, he lowered the barrel, pointing it at the wolf that was now only several feet away. Buck pulled the trigger and watched the animal collapse over its front paws and slide into the mud, coming to a final halt at Buck's feet.

Buck's own head fell back into the mud, and he breathed in for the first time since the attack began. He concentrated on keeping his mind clear for the task ahead. He looked down at his arm. Blood was pouring from a severed artery. He knew the odds were against him being able to tie a tourniquet with one working hand before passing out from loss of blood. He had to get his belt off and wrap it around his bicep.

He propped himself up on his elbow and looked over at the wolf that had surprised him. There, her throat cut, lay Victoria. In the last seconds of death, she had curled herself into the fetal position.

Buck felt the dread wash over him, as he looked away from the girl and down at his feet. His beautiful son's contorted body had replaced that of the wolf. His only child's eyes were open, staring lifeless into Buck's.

Buck woke up to sheets wet with sweat. The fever had started. He turned on the bedside lamp and knocked a photo to the floor, the glass in the frame shattering as it hit.

He fell back onto the pillow and ran his fingers through his damp hair. Then, he sat up, swung his feet over the side of the bed, and, without thinking, stepped onto the broken glass.

"Fuck."

Buck hopped over to the end of the bed, grabbed a t-shirt off the floor, and wrapped it around his foot.

"Great. Now I'm dreaming premonitions."

Buck looked under the t-shirt. The cut wasn't deep. He pulled out a shard of glass, wrapped it in the t-shirt, and then hopped over to his dresser. He opened a drawer and pulled out a medical kit labeled "Please Return to Assistant Director." The irony after the Reverend's comment on stealing almost made Buck smile. He opened the small case and rummaged through band-aids and antibiotic creams and grabbed what he was looking for.

Buck rested his foot on the open drawer and shook a small, blue can. He sprayed liquid onto the bottom of his foot and a quick-drying red film formed over his wound.

He stared at the can.

"Unbelievable."

Buck blew on the artificial skin, then gingerly placed his foot onto the hardwood floor. It still hurt, but at least there was no trail of blood to clean up in the morning.

Buck hobbled out of his bedroom into his dark and silent home. He stopped at his son's room and peered inside. Moonlight fell across Trey's bed. His son's body spooned Victoria's sleeping figure. Well, this was something Buck was just going to have to accept. They sure as hell weren't living with Geraldine. He'd put a stop to that plan.

Buck pulled the door to and walked through the living room to his home's front door. He opened the door, pulled off his shorts, and stood naked in the entranceway. A light breeze cooled the moisture coating his body. He imagined this was what air conditioning felt like.

Buck stepped off his front porch and slipped into the woods just a few feet away. The pine needles felt good against his skin, scratching his constant itch. Buck's mind started to cloud at the same time his instinct began to take over. He could smell the deer. It was very close. His senses were so acute now that he could tell it was a doe. Shame blurred with joy, and both were replaced by the singular need to feed a deep hunger. He ran with the moon. She would satiate his hunger like nothing else could.

Darkly and Gus had arranged to investigate the crime scene themselves at two in the morning, and she had been unable to get any sleep before then. She was overcome with feelings of dread since the inquest. If history was anything to go by, these feelings were not to be taken as insignificant. She tiptoed over to Gus's room. He opened the door before she could knock.

My God, did clouds never obscure the moon in this place? Darkly and Gus looked up at the night sky that revealed their activities almost as clearly as day. She could see a mouse scurry across the street in front of them and disappear down the alleyway. Darkly would have preferred to take a closer look in daylight at the spot where Christopher's body had lain, but that really would have drawn attention. She examined streaks of blood between the service door to the hotel and the dumpster and gave Gus a knowing look.

"He tried to get inside," Gus said as he tried the handle. "It locks automatically from the inside."

He took out a credit card from his wallet and slid it between the lock and door frame. The door opened, and he left it propped open with a rock.

"What do you think about the naked girl, Gus?"

How could Darkly explain to him the death she tasted when she sipped the cup of coffee poured by Victoria?

"The magistrate was pretty quick to attribute it to trauma and a trick of the light. The thing is, nobody heard him scream."

"Fear and shock are a recipe for muteness."

Darkly was keen to see if Gus led this back to Geraldine's slip of the tongue.

"It could also mean he wasn't afraid. At first. He didn't see it coming."

"So, he wasn't scared of bears?"

"People are killed every year at picnic sites, getting too close to wildlife to capture a once-in-a-lifetime photo."

"True. The alternative being--"

"It wasn't a bear."

"Okay. But, what are we talking about here, Darkly? Those weren't knife wounds on the body. If it was a person, how do you explain that?"

"Maybe they brought a large dog with them? Have you ever seen a death from a mastiff attack? I have! It isn't pretty."

Darkly walked around the crime scene and tried to piece the possible scenario together.

"Christopher steps out the back door for fresh air."

"Wouldn't he just use the front door like all the other hotel guests?"

"You'd think, wouldn't you? So, he doesn't want anyone to see him leaving the hotel. Because he was going someplace he shouldn't?"

Gus carried the thought further. "Or he was exactly where he wanted to be. A nice secluded place for a conversation with--"

"A friend. Or at least someone he knew. Someone who knew him by the name--"

"Sam."

Gus was enjoying being on the same page with Darkly. It wasn't the norm for him, as he suspected it wasn't for her.

"So, you're saying that Christopher--"

"Sam."

"Sam came out to meet a naked girl with a dog? She didn't like what he had to say, so she set her dog on him?"

Darkly didn't reply. She was still thinking. Gus continued with his deduction, though.

"So, is the girl a member of the cast or one of the townsfolk? And is she even real? Is Carter making it all up for some reason? Is he involved?"

Gus assaulted Darkly with questions. At least the answer to the girl question was an easy one.

"Town," Darkly answered. "Besides me, Serena is the only woman associated with the film. She didn't bring a dog with her that I know of. And if it had been her, Carter's been around Serena enough to know the way she moves. He would have recognized her and said something to someone. You've observed them all. Have any of them blown you away with their acting skills, let alone the director?"

"What? Who blew the director?"

"Funny."

"Who's to say Carter didn't tell someone?" Gus was back on track.

"But, where does the dog, bear, killer bunny rabbit fit in?"

Darkly and Gus were only creating more questions, not solving them.

"No, I don't believe it was Serena, and yes, I do think Carter was telling the truth about the girl. But, I'm confident that Christopher, or Sam, knew that girl. Which leaves the question as to why she was naked." Darkly wasn't beaten yet.

"There is one reason more plausible than the rest," responded Gus. "She knew Sam really well, and they were caught in the act by a passing bear. She got away, and he didn't. Simple accident of fate."

Before she opened her mouth, Gus knew she thought this explanation implausible at best.

"If it is a simple case of the naked girl who got away because she ran faster, then why doesn't she come forward?" Darkly asked.

"I don't know. She's married?"

"We're talking about a man's death. That trumps infidelity, doesn't it?" At least, Darkly hoped it would.

"In my experiences with small towns, I'd have to say no."

Gus started to chuckle, but was cut off by Darkly's intent study of the dumpster.

"What are you thinking?"

"Let's go with the Gus theory, Gus."

"I never said I have a theory yet."

"Okay then. Let's go with the Gus hypothesis that he's about five percent committed to. Sam arranges to meet a local girl in back alley. Either he'd been to this town before or charmed her when we weren't looking. He gets her clothes off, while remaining fully clothed himself. That's odd, don't you think?"

"Again, from my experience--"

"They're interrupted by a grizzly, jealous husband, or Cujo. She runs off scared out of her wits and keeps her mouth shut. So, where are her clothes, Gus?"

Gus didn't have to be asked twice. He lifted open the rusty, creaky lid to the dumpster, throwing it back with some effort. The loud bang of metal against metal set off a domino effect of dogs barking. Gus and Darkly held their breaths and standstill position for what felt like an eternity. If Darkly's looks could kill, Christopher wouldn't have been the only person to see his life end in this alleyway.

Several minutes later, the barking dissipated, and Gus climbed inside. Darkly turned on her flashlight and shone it down into the steel box.

It was disgusting. Lewis was clearly using the dumpster for compost because Gus found himself standing in thigh-high egg shells, moldy bread, leaves and old grease.

"You're forgiven," Darkly said cheerfully.

She scanned the muck until her light picked up a corner of something white poking up out of the organic sludge. Gus grunted as he stuck his hand into the stew. What he pulled out was a woman's blouse, ripped at the seams. Wrapped inside the blouse, was a knife with an unusual blade.

Gus held the blade under Darkly's light.

"The handle's made of bone. Not sure about the blade. Maybe pewter?"

Darkly pressed a finger to the blade and felt the electrical vibration run up her hand and into her wrist.

"It's pure silver."

And so Darkly made another trip to examine a body, in hopes that questions would give way to revelations. Remaining as much under cover of shadow as they could, Darkly and Gus made their way to church.

Gus had taken a closer look at the town that day, under the guise of photographing the quaint surroundings. He captured Buck and his son transporting Christopher's body to the church basement in preparation for burial.

The sanctuary's stained glass windows were dark at this hour, but the windows of the basement, whose panes opened at the level of the grass yard, were brimming with light.

The sound of boots trudging through soggy ground made their way up the church yard. Darkly and Gus crouched behind a holly bush, doing their best not to prick themselves on the thorny leaves. The boots stopped a few feet from the bush. Darkly heard a key slide into a lock, and a small door open. The light from the basement illuminated the churchyard for a moment threatening to reveal their hiding spot, but the soles of the boots smacked the solid stone inside, unaware of the hidden observers.

Darkly acted quickly and slid on her belly, reaching from under the bush to grab the base of the door before it shut. She crept up onto her feet and peered in through the crack of the door. A lit, empty passageway led down stone steps to hanging, thick, red curtains.

Darkly gave Gus a silent hand gesture telling him to remain where he was. He didn't look pleased, as she made her way inside and let the door shut behind her. She slipped off her shoes and proceeded silently down to the curtains. She grabbed hold of the dusty satin and pulled apart the two panels just enough to see but not be seen.

The room was the typical church basement hall. Classroom chairs lined the walls like they would at a school dance. A small stage and lectern was positioned below the pulpit of the sanctuary above. In one corner, Darkly saw the gathering of men. All had been present at the inquest. Reverend MacIntyre stood among them, studying a pocket watch in his hand. The men encircled a coffin perched on top of a sturdy, oak table. The casket was a charcoal black with pewter handles.

MacIntyre looked up from the watch.

"Where's the sheriff?"

No one answered him. MacIntyre looked at the curtains. Darkly closed the panels and held her breath. After thirty seconds and no movement from within the room, she dared to look again.

One of the townsmen rested his ear on the coffin lid. He raised his head and looked at one of the other men.

"Will it hold?"

The other man took offense in his reply. "I've been a carpenter all my life."

"I'm sure that no doubt in your skills was intended, George," MacIntyre intervened.

The coffin suddenly shifted several inches, and the men leapt back with surprise. Darkly distinctly heard the sound of wood cracking. The men looked at George for reassurance. He looked concerned.

"It'll hold. That was just the inner casket. The outer one's lined with lead."

"We should have burned him by now."

One of the other men kept a greater distance than the rest. MacIntyre maintained his nerve.

"His sins are great. But we wait it out as agreed."

Darkly thought she could hear a low growl emanate from the coffin, as the hand reached over her head and silenced her scream.

CHAPTER THIRTEEN

Darkly caught site of the holly bush from the passenger seat of Buck's truck. Gus was gone. The sheriff sat with his hands on the steering wheel and his eyes locked on the church basement windows.

Buck didn't look at Darkly while he questioned her.

"Why were you spying on the mourners?"

"What was *I* doing? Mourners? What the hell were *they* doing? And what's with all the cloak and dagger? From where I'm sitting, you were spying on me. You couldn't simply tap me on the shoulder?"

"We keep the old traditions alive in this town."

"Stalking?"

Buck looked genuinely taken aback by the suggestion that he had taken a liberty with Darkly.

"Mourners stand watch over the deceased the night before burial. A 19th Century precaution against narcolepsy. I was trying to save you any embarrassment from being discovered. Spying. On a sacred observance."

Darkly wasn't buying it.

"Narcolepsy, huh? Well, that coffin moved. That's one active dead guy."

Buck looked Darkly in the eye for the first time that night.

"You imagined it," Buck said, as he started the truck engine. "I'll drive you back to your hotel."

"Who's in that coffin?"

"Your friend, Christopher. You saw for yourself that he is very much dead."

"Those men in there didn't seem so sure about that."

"What are you saying? We bury people alive for fun?"

Darkly knew what she saw. She wasn't crazy. But, she wasn't so sure she had nothing to fear from Buck. She decided to put self-preservation above indignation.

"My imagination could have gotten carried away."

Buck was silent for a couple moments before responding.

"It has to be stressful for all of you. You're so far away from home, and something like this happens. I can only imagine. Residual electric impulses can trigger in the brain many hours after death. I've seen it myself. That could explain what you saw."

"You mean what I thought I saw?"

Why did Darkly find it so hard to contain her sarcasm when she knew it was in her own best interest to do so?

Buck pulled up outside the hotel's front doors. He didn't have time to put the truck in park before Darkly had leapt out the passenger door.

"Thanks for the lift. I'll see you at the funeral tomorrow."

Just before Darkly could close the door, Buck called out to her, "You can tell your friend hiding in the bed of my truck that he can get out now. I'd hate to see him get hurt jumping from a moving vehicle."

Darkly walked alongside the bed of the truck and slapped the side hard a couple of times.

Gus poked his head up and looked at Buck scowling at him from the rear view mirror.

The fact that Darkly fell asleep after the night's adventure was a miracle. The fact that she hadn't been asleep for more than half an hour when shots rang out through the night didn't surprise her in the least. It took a moment to realize they were shots. In her dream, she was only three, riding her tricycle down a steep hill. The houses at the bottom were the size of ants. As the cycle picked up speed, her feet pedaled too fast. She had to fling them up into the air and rely on just the steering. The small tire at the front blew out, then the small back right tire, and finally the left. Little Darkly went flying into the air. She became a bird, a raven, and the houses below were no longer ants, but specks of dust on a white ball of snow. Then she was falling through the sky. Black feathers scattered themselves across the white ground.

The gunshots that rang in the now very much awake ears of Darkly Stewart competed with the banging at her door.

"Darkly! Please, can I come in?"

It was a very scared Serena on the other side of the door.

Darkly got out of bed and dislodged the chair from its position under the doorknob. A sensible precaution. She unlocked and opened the door and was nearly thrown to the ground when Serena grabbed hold of her and squeezed the breath out of her.

"I couldn't wake the guys. Didn't you hear it? The guns? The bear is back! It likes how we taste now. We can't go outside ever again. We're trapped!"

Darkly extricated herself from Serena's embrace, while being careful to keep hold of the frightened girl's hand. The two moved as one entity to the window and peered down into the street below.

Fog had rolled in from the mountains, but below her window, Darkly could see the men from the church basement hovering over a lanky, silver wolf. Blood poured from the wolf's mouth onto the cobbles of the street that marked its final stand.

Out of the mist, Buck approached the kill, his rifle smoking in the cool night air.

Serena left Darkly's side and collapsed onto the bed. Terror melted into relief, and she curled up into a ball. She was clearly not going back to her room tonight. Darkly stepped away from the window for a few seconds to cover Serena in a blanket.

She returned to the window intent on calling out to Buck to congratulate him on catching Christopher's killer: a wolf, not a bear. She stopped herself on the cusp of reveal and sank back into the room.

Where there had been a wolf lying dead on the cold, damp stone, there was now a man. It was Christopher. He was whole with his injuries from the night before healed, except for the trickle of blood that now ran down the corner of his mouth.

Darkly climbed onto the bed and wrapped herself around Serena, who was falling back into the protection of sleep. For Darkly, there was no such solace. She knew now she had to get out of this town. They all did. Their lives depended on it.

CHAPTER FOURTEEN

Buck had been careless. He knew that. He could lay the blame at no one's feet but his own. His authority rested in his ability to prevent violence and to preserve the viability of the town's population. The one saving grace was that Sam had brought mainly men with him. Too many of the females of the town had been waiting for this opportunity.

Part of him genuinely felt bad about what awaited the visitors. Perhaps never to see the ones they love again. Wolf Woods was a prison to him, and he was his own warden. He could only imagine what it would be like to those who drank from the well of freedom every day of their lives.

Then, there was Darkly. She smelled familiar. Was there some distant cousin many hundreds of times removed in her bloodline? But how could that be? They were the last. The Inquisition had taken all but that small boatload of pilgrims who had escaped to Scotland and then eventually the New World. The great betrayal took most of those.

His ancestors had taken their revenge on the French, the great-grandsons of those men who had ravaged village after village, ripping babies from mothers' wombs, burning whole families together at the stake, and forcing fathers to watch children set upon by baited bears.

How quickly their enemies had forgotten the past when Buck's kind had repelled the Mongol hoards and then the Turks. Buck's ancestors had saved Europe time and time again, and then received the decimation of their bloodlines as payment. But now, thanks to the plan recently set in motion, the tables would be turned. The damned would bring damnation to all, and thus all would be saved.

The Plains of Abraham floated above the British encampments. The torches of the sentries stood guard alongside the stars as the lesser lights of the dark sky. The solution was genius. General James Wolfe had gambled the French would never suspect an entire army could be moved up a small cliff-side path. And at the vanguard of that army was the great-great-grandfather of Buck's great-great-grandfather. Nathaniel Mordecai Robertson would extinguish the insufficient sentries that dotted the pathway before they even knew he was there.

Onto the rocks below, the bones and brains of these young men in their brilliant blue tunics were dashed to pieces. By morning, Wolfe lay dying, but the war's outcome was secured.

Nathaniel's deadly service had been bought with the hand of his daughter to the newly-promoted General William Howe in secret matrimony, along with the promise of a homeland for Nathaniel's people, where they could live free of persecution. Yet, once again, the children of Nebadchanezar faced betrayal. By the fire of the burning French homes, General Howe slit his new bride's throat and ordered that all such abominations of God be cut down with silver blades.

Buck caught himself mumbling curses at the unfortunate course of history, as he lifted Sam's body off the bed of his truck and carried the dead man to the mine shaft. It was to avoid such slaughter that Buck had restricted the keeping of silver bullets to the sheriff alone. Would his successor follow his example or allow the town to descend into the violence of former times? If he could see his son take his place, then perhaps more dangerous elements would be kept in check. As they were tonight. But, even then, Geraldine had become the kingmaker by ensuring Victoria was now, in effect, Buck's daughter.

Buck placed Sam's body on the ground and grabbed hold of one of the boards he had placed over the mine opening a couple days before. Once he had pulled enough boards free, he grabbed hold of Sam's ankles and dragged the body, hunched over and backwards, into the tomb. He would learn soon enough what it was Sam had been so desperate to meet with him about. What threat Sam had seen in the outside world.

Darkly slid the last note under Carter's door. Peter and Shane would wake to find the same instructions. She sat by her window and watched the sky turn from black to pale blue, as Serena slept contentedly a few feet away.

At sunrise, Gus entered without a word. Shane was the first of the actors to knock. He was wearing his sweats, and Darkly was glad to see he showed up at her door before he went for his run. Peter and Carter were a half hour behind.

"Early morning. This time tomorrow is best, when the townspeople are at their groggiest. We leave in two vehicles and abandon the trailers."

Darkly felt honesty was the best policy at this point. All the Little Red Riding Hoods should abandon the trip to grandmother's house and get the hell out of the woods.

"I don't understand. We all saw the body, Darkly," said Carter.

Carter looked like death warmed over. This latest enterprise was going to seal the deal with his father. He'd be banished to some middle-management position in a regional office like Kansas City, and his life would be over.

"Parts of him were eaten," Carter said, as though no one else had noticed that grim fact.

"Are you saying I imagined what I saw?" Darkly responded.

"That's exactly what he's saying. It's what I'm saying too. None of us liked Christopher all that much, but this is in bad taste," reprimanded Shane.

Shane had said his peace and now got up to leave. Serena reached out for Darkly.

"I believe you."

"Hold on, Shane." Carter went into director mode. "None of this matters. I've decided to shut down production. We can pull out by the end of day tomorrow."

Peter looked ready to object, but Carter cut him off.

"I will honor all contracts. With the money saved by pulling the plug, artists' fees can be covered in full. I'll let the sheriff know at the funeral today."

"No," said Darkly. "Don't say anything to anyone."

Darkly realized she was going to have to pull out the big guns.

"Who the hell do you think you are?"

Peter stood up and got in her face. Gus moved to her side, but she waved him aside. She knew how to take care of this once and for all. Darkly emptied her pack onto her bed, tore back the bottom nylon panel and pulled out the hidden RCMP badge.

It was now Gus's turn to get in Peter's face.

"And in case you were wondering, photography isn't my main gig either."

"I'm with Officer Darkly. You should be too," pleaded Serena.

"Constable," corrected Darkly.

"Constable Darkly," Serena said with a shaking voice brought on by a body that was also shaking. She was a bundle of nerves. She should probably take another pill. It would have a calming effect.

"I have people to thank and pay," Carter protested.

"Leave a note and a cheque by your bedside."

Carter and Darkly stared at one another until Serena broke the silence.

"Should we get breakfast? Won't it look suspicious if we don't?"

"I'm not hungry," said Carter, who left without saying another word.

Serena smiled and said with the glee of a schoolgirl, "Yay. We're going home."

But not until tomorrow. Darkly knew a lot could happen in a day. And wolves run in packs.

The clouds rolled in an hour before the funeral. Buck took his position as a pallbearer. Carter, Darkly, Gus and the actors stood around the open grave under the overcast sky.

The pressure in Buck's skull told him they were in for a downpour later.

A few local onlookers were still showing up to pay their respects.

The coffin was set down onto two-by-fours in front of Reverend MacIntyre, his bible open at the ready. The official mourners Darkly had observed previously grabbed the ends to the two ropes that lay beside the boards supporting the coffin's weight. Upon lifting the coffin, Buck pulled the boards out of the way, and it was lowered into the grave.

Darkly noticed the coffin's lid was splintered in parts, but patched back together and messily painted over. She even noticed a hanging hinge. But, she had been looking for imperfections.

The grave-side sermon was the traditional ashes to ashes, dust to dust, with a smattering of the mystery of God's ways. Geraldine, Trey, and Victoria were also in attendance. Geraldine's face displayed momentary outbreaks of joy. And when she invited Carter and the rest back to the diner for post-burial refreshments, her look of sadness resembled something from a French mime's act.

This whole situation was getting out of hand. This kind of glee was contagious and soon the whole town would catch the scent. Buck looked at his boy. He was forced to acknowledge that Victoria made him happy. Buck loved his son more than anything or anyone else in this world. Today was the day to preserve a future for him and his descendants.

The Moon River Diner was filled to capacity. A social event, even one as dour as a funeral, was a break from the monotony that appeared a constant in Wolf Woods.

Buck helped himself to a deviled egg and caught Carter's eye in the corner of the room. He could make out the director's conversation with Ed. It was something about big screen televisions hanging on the living room walls of every American home. Ed was bewildered. This was it. "Here we go," Buck said under his breath.

Ed saw Buck's approach and walked away without excusing himself.

"Got a moment?" asked Buck.

Carter watched Ed walk off and inhale a pork pie like a grape. "Interesting guy."

"Yeah. We aren't lacking for characters in this town. You folks could make a movie about each one of them, if you were so inclined."

"I wish I could. The thing is, I think this is me done with moviemaking. The gods have spoken, and I've finally decided to listen.

"I see. So, what's your plan for this film?"

Carter had thought about what Darkly said, but he also knew he was a dreadful liar. And even if she was a Mountie, Carter was convinced that old Hollywood adage of nobody knows anything about anything held true for the world of cops too. So, he told Buck he was pulling the plug.

"We'll pull out by tomorrow night."

"I see." Time for Buck's sales pitch. "I'm not going to lie to you, Carter. We are a town in decline. We could sure use a shot in the arm from the outside world. We need teachers for our young, leaders who can turn this place around. We used to be quite a vibrant place. I believe we could be again with the help of good, talented folks like you."

"I'm sorry?" Carter was flattered and confused. "You want me to, what, take up part-time residence as a professor or something?"

"No, I'm asking you to move here permanently. All of you."

Carter laughed. "No offence, Sheriff, but we all have lives we put on hold. If you're looking to set up a sort of mountain film center like Sundance, well, yeah, I could consider some kind of consulting role."

"I don't know what Sundance is, but I'd like to show you something, if I may."

Buck glanced at Doc Ross, who nodded his head.

"Okay."

Carter was finding this incredibly bizarre. His movie goes down the toilet, a cast member gets eaten by a bear, or wolf, and this civil servant thinks he'd like to hang around for a few years.

Buck unbuttoned the top two buttons of his shirt. Carter assumed this was going to be a display of battle scars or tattoos. Carter had not so much as a dog bite or the word *Mom* on his body, so there was really no point in showing up to this competition.

Carter smiled and looked into Buck's eyes. There was something suddenly different about the man. His clear slate blue eyes were changing right in front of Carter. The blood vessels in the whites of the sheriff's eyes became engorged. A wave of mustard yellow seeped into the corneas, a muddy pond replacing the sea that was there a moment before. Buck stepped out of the loafers he'd put on specifically for the funeral.

Carter watched, amazed, as Buck's face twitched, and his hands clasped a chair next to him. His fingers were retracting into his palms just as the nails were growing. Carter now thought backing up to be a very good idea. No one else had noticed yet.

Buck still felt lucid. His feet were expanding through his socks now. He didn't expect Victoria learned anything about darning from her mother. He felt the cold floor against the bare pads of his feet. He looked over at Doc Ross.

Doc reached into his pocket and pulled out a small pistol. He nodded his head at Buck and smiled comfortingly. Good old Doc.

Serena noticed the pistol first, and followed Doc's gaze over to Buck. She screamed just as Buck dropped to all fours and felt the wave of nausea pass over him, to be replaced with the heat running through the capillaries under his skin. He looked up at Carter, who had pressed himself against the wall behind him. His eyes were fixed on Buck. He was frozen in terror.

The townsfolk in the diner each stepped into place next to one of the film people. It was choreographed like a ballet. Geraldine sidled up to Darkly and put her arm around the younger woman's waist.

Darkly tore her eyes away from Buck for a moment. Geraldine smiled with a "such is life" look smeared across her face.

Darkly watched the scene unfold and was once again a little girl hiding from monsters. The long-repressed memory of her biological mother's face flashed before her eyes. A woman in torment, a woman transforming, just as the man in front of her was doing. Darkly clutched her necklace, stroking it for comfort.

Geraldine stroked Darkly's hair.

"Don't be afraid. All is as it should be."

Darkly didn't notice Geraldine's smile turn to a frown when she looked down at Darkly's chest and saw the blue veins showing through the make-up Darkly had not touched up this morning.

"What a beautiful necklace, you have there. Where did you get it?"

Darkly didn't hear her.

Buck's shirt and pants tore open, as his shoulders and hindquarters expanded. His ears had climbed up onto the front of his head, and his mouth had become a snout of long, yellowed teeth. The wolf was the size of Buck, just differently proportioned, wiry, and covered in long, coarse brown hair.

Buck's eyes had not left the petrified Carter. He snarled, and placed one paw in front of the other, ready to devour the director. Or so Carter thought.

The truth was, there were two kinds of werewolves. All lost most of their identity in the transformation. But, they did not forget their humanity. In fact, a few, like Buck, had spent years working at maintaining more than a tenuous link to their human consciousness. Regardless, in the wolf state, it was a deep-rooted instinct to be wary of attack by humans they encountered. Snarling and growling were defensive measures meant to scare off the threat. Nothing more.

But, the second kind of werewolf, unlike Buck, saw humans as prey. Sam was the second kind, just like Buck's brother Wyatt.

Buck believed Victoria was inclined to be, as well. For the sake of Trey, he held out hope that she would grow out of it.

Doc fired the pistol. Buck yelped as the dart lodged itself under one of his shoulder blades. One more step, and the animal collapsed. The wolf strained to lift its head off the floor and turned to look directly at Darkly. They were Buck's eyes as much as the wolf's. There was a human soul in there. Buried, but in there, nonetheless. Darkly had seen it.

Buck slid his snout under his paw in one final defensive gesture, and then passed from consciousness. No one said a word, as Ed came forward and hoisted the wolf over his shoulders and carried Buck out of The Moon River Diner. The wolf had already begun the transformation back to man.

CHAPTER FIFTEEN

Buck knew it was wrong. But wrong where? In the outside world, sure it was. But here? This was self-preservation. He was protecting her interests as much as his own. If not him, someone else. And he knew she liked him. She came here of her own free will, after all.

He slid his hand across Darkly's beautiful body, moving down under the sheets, trailing his mouth across her own at the exact moment he slid his fingers inside her. She didn't resist. He accepted her permission and took her upper lip between his own lips. As he bit down softly, Darkly moved her hands over his buttocks and pulled him closer, asking for more of him. She could not contain herself. This was all so much more than desire.

Darkly let go of Buck and grabbed the bed sheet in his stead. Her nails passed through the fabric and dug deep indentations into her palms. Buck wanted her. He wanted her all at once. It was that overwhelming need to claim her so that no one else could.

He forced himself to slow his pace. He became gentler. He looked down into her open eyes, and she smiled up at him. She ran her fingers through his hair and pulled his mouth back to hers. There was no turning back now.

It had been so very long for Buck. This kind of intimacy was for other men. He had to forgo so much for the good of the rest. Well, that is what he told himself. There had certainly been no lack of offers. There were the casual drop-bys with a cake. Those young women soon gave up hope. There were the dirty looks from the ancient women. Who was he to put the future of the town at risk by acting like some old spinster? But he was raising Trey. Trey would be his only focus. He would not be distracted from the task at hand. Trey would lead this town into a better age when Buck was gone.

He had saved the infant's life, a new life that would have been denied his birth rite in the outside world. And now his beautiful son was one of them, one of the damned. Yet, he was damned and happy. Trey and Victoria ran through the night together, bound up in something greater together than they could experience separately.

There had been similar nights of a purely physical nature for Buck. He would find himself chasing the white light in the sky. Then, suddenly, another moon runner was flying through the night alongside of him. Vague memories of biting the back of her neck, and that merciful release. It was never spoken of the next day. Sometimes, the scent of another gave it away, and he and the young woman would avoid each other's gaze for a week or two. Even among monsters, there was a sense of propriety.

Buck turned Darkly over onto her stomach. He kissed the back of her neck and breathed in deeply the scent of her hair. Darkly turned her head, and Buck followed her gaze out the bedroom window. The sliver of a crescent of moon was disappearing beyond the window frame. It was setting almost as fast as the sun. The sun was, in fact, set, but its residual light clung to the horizon like a child fighting sleep. That light, that mere memory of the day, grabbed hold of the moon, as if to pull the graceful lady unwillingly into bed, and stained her with blood in the struggle. The moon was bleeding. It was just like that evening two decades ago.

Wyatt had spotted them first. There hadn't been campers up there on the ridge in a few years. He said there was a couple. No one suspected it was the last of the Darkly family who had returned.

Sheriff Luther called a meeting of the town elders. Wyatt and Buck's father hated what were referred to as "events." But there was no denying the desperate nature of their situation. Five babies had died this past winter, genetically weakened to the usual line-up of infant illnesses. The town needed new blood. Its days were numbered.

From the first days of the curse, many had argued the best thing for their kind *would* be to die out. They were, after all, an abomination. But, how could any father deny his children the hope of redemption, however faint that hope may be? So, they kept producing one generation after the next. But they had a new plan brewing. A plan that would eventually end centuries of isolation.

It was decided. The campers would be taken. The man would have to be killed. Sadly, Luther knew there was no way around this. And he knew his son was all too willing to carry out the dreaded deed. Luther told himself it was because Wyatt was ready to accept such duties to spare others the awful responsibility. But, Luther also knew, deep down, that this was a lie.

They had tried to reach accommodations with couples in the past, but discovered a clean break was the only chance for a female captive's adjustment to the reality of a very difficult situation. The women of the town would help her as best they could. But, even then, the possibility of suicide was still high.

It was Luther's duty as the Alpha, the sheriff of the town, to supervise all such events. He was also training his son to be ready for his own bid for the position. So, tonight, Wyatt would lead the abduction, and Luther would pore himself a whisky and wait at home. It was a test that Luther's son would fail.

Buck woke from the dream on Doc's hard examination table. There was no Darkly beside him. He was alone, naked and covered with a sheet. On Doc's desk, there was a change of clothes and a piece of chocolate cake.

After the revelation at the diner, Darkly and the others were escorted back to the hotel under armed guard. They found Marvin and Jake had been brought into town to join them, and that good old boys stood guard with shotguns at the front desk. A plate of egg salad sandwiches sat undisturbed in front of them.

Marvin looked up at Darkly as she entered the foyer. He had returned to set after the funeral to prepare for closing up shop and clearly knew nothing about what had taken place earlier in the day. Darkly looked away, having no clue what to say. Nothing could adequately describe the day's events.

Lewis strolled up to the group and eyed the untouched plate of sandwiches and shook his head.

"Doc will be around later," he said.

Lewis was holding a stack of old National Geographics. He placed them on the table next to the plate of sandwiches and noticed there were two more people than he had originally made up rooms for. Marvin and Jake had been staying in the RVs at night. He was not about to beat the dust out of another bed.

"The Reverend thought you might want something to read. Some of you might have to double up tonight."

He shook his head again and walked back to the front desk, not at all happy to have customers.

Doc Ross arrived late in the afternoon. His general disposition was cheery. He wore a tweed jacket and looked as benign as anyone who isn't capable of growing hair and fangs on command.

He slapped Carter on the back and reached into the group and pulled out a sandwich of now wilted lettuce and egg more brown than yellow. He took a bite.

"Whichever one of you is lucky enough to get Lucy, you won't go hungry."

"Excuse me?" Peter asked, agitated and pacing the hotel foyer.

Doc smiled and pulled out an old pipe from his pocket. The mouthpiece was indented with teeth marks. He looked into the empty bowl.

"I don't suppose one of you has any tobacco?" Doc asked hopefully.

The group looked at him blankly.

"A cigarette will do."

Peter stopped his pacing and pulled a pack of Marlboros from his pocket and presented it to Doc Ross.

"I'll give you the whole fucking pack if you call off the redneck posse and let me the hell out of here."

Doc leveled his eyes at Peter. He took the pack of cigarettes, removed one, and handed the pack back to Peter.

"Just the one will do. I may be a doctor, but I have no desire to deny a man his little vices."

Doc removed a silver lighter from his pocket and lit the cigarette. He closed his eyes and shuddered, his hand shaking as it touched the silver. He lit the cigarette and savored the first drag.

"It reminds me of my cross to bear."

Doc held the lighter out for all to see before putting it back in his pocket. After the brief moments of elation the cigarette brought, Doc reopened his eyes and addressed the whole group.

"I must explain. Lupinism, that is, the act of becoming a werewolf, is a condition contracted through sexual intercourse. There is no cure that has yet been discovered. There are those of us who have come to look at things from the opposite perspective. Perhaps becoming a werewolf is a cure for the disease of being merely human. It is in this belief you must place your trust if you ever wish to leave this town again."

Buck, Doc Ross, Geraldine, and Reverend MacIntyre sat around the diner table. Geraldine reached into the center of the table and grabbed the coffee pot. She began topping up four cups.

"This is the last of the coffee. It's back to home-grown garden mint tea, unless one of our scouts could put it on the shopping list."

"It can't be a priority," Buck explained. "Not when we're so low on essential medicines."

The remaining amount Geraldine was going to pour into Buck's cup, she now poured into her own.

"Is that supposed to teach me a lesson?" Buck quipped.

"Could you two try to behave like the leaders of the community you are?" Reverend MacIntyre scolded.

The Reverend had known both Buck and Geraldine from the time they were cubs, and he had never seen them miss an opportunity to take a jab at one another.

"You both really do try my God-given patience at times."

Buck and Geraldine looked down at the table in remorse. Buck sipped his empty cup.

Doc Ross took over.

"Thank you, Reverend." So, we need to decide who mates with who.

The good Reverend butted in again. "Arranged marriages, if you please, Doctor."

"If that helps, all right," Doc continued. "Who marries who? This is the best of any situation. Six eligible bachelors, and two young women of the right age."

Doc Ross looked down at a list of names.

"So, we have fifteen women who have been patiently waiting for just such an opportunity. I suggest we arrange a good old-fashioned mixer and let nature run its course."

"You mean dancing?" Reverend MacIntyre asked with a twinkle in his eye.

Buck smiled. He knew of the Reverend's weakness for a waltz. How times had changed. In Buck's youth, when they were forced to recruit from the outside world, it was women who were needed. Now, the tables had turned.

"Good," Doc Ross said. "Reverend MacIntyre has kindly agreed to host the dance in the church basement."

"And what about the women?" Geraldine asked.

"What do you think Geraldine? You're the only woman at the table."

Doc Ross was genuinely willing to defer to her judgment.

"Thank you for noticing, Doc. We all know the problem the Darkly girl presents. Curious, nosey. Ed is a forceful man."

"Force of nature more like it," the Reverend snorted.

"He could bring her into line." Geraldine smiled at Buck when she said this.

"It does seem only fair. He's been passed up--" Doc Ross began.

"I'll take her." Buck looked ready to leap on the table and proclaim it to the world.

The rest of the table sat there in silence for a moment, rather stunned.

Geraldine broke the silence. "You already have a son."

"As you have said to me before, I have a son, but I never produced one."

"And God loves you for what you did, my boy."

Reverend MacIntyre was unsuccessful in breaking the tension.

"Buck, you have had the opportunity to take any woman in the town. It's your right--"

"And I am now exercising that right," Buck answered Doc Ross. "Give the other girl to Ed."

Doc Ross nodded his head.

"I believe Darkly's already with the photographer," Geraldine retorted.

"Then we'll have to split them up," Buck said with uncharacteristic lack of sympathy in his voice. "She'll adjust."

Buck got up from the table, effectively ending the meeting of the town council. He tipped his hat to the table and walked out of the diner.

Geraldine smiled brightly at the two remaining men.

"My goodness, the sheriff never ceases to surprise me. Doc, your grandson, Zachariah, he enjoys his first moon run tonight, doesn't he?"

"Yes he does, Geraldine."

"Such a big day in any young boy's life. Or girl's life. I remember my own. You tell him I'm going to bake a big gooseberry pie in his honor."

Carter was now explaining to Jake and Marvin the unbelievable course of events that meant they were all screwed. Darkly could hear muffled yelling through the wall dividing her room and Carter's. The talk wasn't going well.

The yelling was abruptly cut off by a quick succession of knocks at Darkly's door. Darkly didn't answer it right away.

"Who is it?"

"It's the sheriff. Buckwald. I mean Buck."

Buck looked down the hallway. Several doors had opened a crack, and people were watching him, making him feel self-conscious.

"Would you mind coming to the door?"

An old fairy tale ran across Darkly's mind.

"Why don't you huff and puff and blow the door down?"

Buck had no clue what she was talking about. He raised a picnic basket into the air, which Darkly couldn't see through the closed door.

"I brought some food. I thought you might be hungry."

Well, Darkly was, indeed, hungry. She had passed on the egg salad sandwiches downstairs.

Buck decided to go through the menu.

"I have egg salad sandwiches, some homemade beer, fruit."

The door opened, and Darkly let it swing wide open.

"I also brought a pie," finished Buck.

"Is it an egg salad pie?"

"No. It's cherry."

"For the record, Sheriff, I hate egg salad. Most people hate egg salad. Are you trying to starve us as well as hold us against our wills?"

"W--we have a lot of chickens."

"I didn't think wolves and chickens got along."

Buck was wearing a crisp white shirt and a tie. His jeans had a pressed crease in them.

"You're thinking of foxes."

They both stood there in silence for a couple of minutes.

"Did I mention I brought beer, which will be cold or warm depending on how long you leave me standing here?"

Darkly let him in and shut the door behind him, prompting Gus to step out of his room and into the hallway. He walked slowly to Darkly's door and pressed his ear to it.

Darkly pointed to the rickety wooden table in the corner.

"You can put it down there."

Buck did as he was told and opened the basket. He removed two mismatched glasses and a tall brown bottle of ale. He removed the twist top and poured him and Darkly some of his homemade concoction. He turned around to pass Darkly her beer. She met the gesture with her RCMP badge held at face level.

"Buckwald Robertson, I'm arresting you for kidnapping. You have the right to retain and instruct counsel without delay. You have the right to keep your mouth shut. Do you wish to make a telephone call?"

"To where?"

"I'm assuming you have a lawyer in this town?"

"We do. But, I don't think his licence is valid any longer."

Buck took a sip of beer.

"I must instruct you to hand your duties over to a deputy."

Buck took another sip.

"I'm afraid I don't have one. But, you've made me realize I should make it a priority. Maybe you'd like to apply for the job?"

Buck held Darkly's beer out to her again. She accepted it and took a long drink out of frustration.

"If you'd like to interrogate me now, I'm happy to answer any questions."

Buck took a seat.

"I'll take a slice of pie now," Darkly demanded.

"Yes ma'am."

Darkly had finished off half the pie before she stopped eating. She picked up the large brown bottle and washed it down with what was left inside. Darkly sat by the window, keeping an eye on the two guards with hunting rifles who patrolled the area around the hotel.

"You look a little different than when I last saw you," Darkly said.

She knew the attempted arrest was a long-shot, especially with a country sheriff. But, she had to try. Now, she might as well learn as much as she could. One thing she already knew. Buck tasted of death. But, then she did see him kill Christopher, or whatever the hell his actual name was. The question was, had he killed before? She fired her opening shot.

"Who is Sam?"

Buck sighed. "I figured you were too smart to accept my cover. Sam was Christopher."

"He was one of you? Your kind?"

"A werewolf? Yes. He grew up here."

"Why did you kill him? Twice?"

Buck shifted in his seat. This was where the explanations became tricky.

"I killed him once. My bullet was the final death. Victoria killed him the first time. She used a silver knife, but she missed the heart. She turned briefly to wolf in order to make it look like an animal attack. But, as I just said, she missed. He healed and lived to die another day."

"You don't seem to miss him."

"He was a killer. Of innocent people."

"Aren't you all killers?

"No more than you are."

"I find that a bit far-fetched. At the diner, you were intent on ordering a Carter burger off the menu."

"It may have seemed like that to you. I may have even hurt him a little if I hadn't been tranquilized, which by the way, I ordered. But, I wouldn't have killed him."

"How can you be so sure?" asked an incredulous Darkly.

"Because I've been this thing my whole life, Darkly, and I swore an oath to protect."

Buck got up and walked to the window.

"I'd like to show you something."

"You mean I'm allowed field trips?"

Geraldine waited until Buck and Darkly had gotten into Buck's truck. Then she entered the hotel. She stopped to look in a mirror and practiced a couple dramatic sighs and worried expressions. She looked over at the table of sandwiches and the flies buzzing around the plate. She curled her lips in disgust. She then called out to Lewis, who came running.

"What is it? Is everything all right? Is there a leak? Is there a fire?" asked the frantic little man.

"Lewis, don't be a fool. When has there ever been any of those things?"

"1961. A fire took the granary. The whole town smelled of popcorn for a fortnight."

"Lewis, shut up. What room is the one named Gus in?"

Lewis looked back at the wooden mail slots. He reached into one and pulled out a folded piece of paper. He read it silently, refolded and put back in the square. He repeated this exercise four times, then looked up at Geraldine.

"Room two sixteen."

She ran the rest of the way to Gus's room, ensuring she looked the part of being out of breath. She then knocked on the door as quietly as she could. Gus opened the door.

"Darkly? Where have you been? Oh." It wasn't Darkly.

Geraldine moved in close, and Gus backed up into a self-defense pose in the middle of his room.

"You have to come with me," Geraldine whispered. "Darkly's in trouble."

Geraldine turned to leave.

"Come quick or it will be too late to save her."

So, Gus did the sensible thing and ran after Geraldine.

CHAPTER SIXTEEN

They'd been sitting in the same spot for almost three hours. The sun had mostly set, but it still held on to the horizon like a stubborn child who would not go to sleep. The deep blue of the sky ahead and the golden grass of the field below Darkly were streaked with pink. It was windy, and the tall grass below the hillside, where Darkly and Buck sat, moved in waves like a body of water.

A cold front was moving in, threatening to turn summer to autumn for the night. Darkly shook slightly from the last impact of wind. Buck removed his jacket and hung it around Darkly's shoulders.

"Here, I'm warm-blooded. I was actually feeling too hot."

"I'm sure."

"It's true. The body temperature of someone like me, well, it runs hotter. A hundred and one degrees Fahrenheit."

"That's the same as a domestic dog, isn't it?" Darkly asked, delighted with her knowledge of trivia.

"We can't be domesticated."

"Why did you bring me here? What did you want to show me?"

Darkly was going to be thoroughly pissed off if this was only some gazing at the sunset romantic gesture. And what exactly was she going to do to communicate she was pissed off? What could she do that would show up someone with his horrific talents?

Then she saw the boy. He looked about twelve or thirteen, with shockingly red hair. Darkly watched his head bounce up and down in the grass like a red buoy on the ocean.

"That's Zachariah." Buck anticipated her question.

"What's he doing?"

"It's his first moon run. The first time he kills."

Buck caught Darkly's look.

"Deer, Darkly, deer. Before now, his parents always killed for him and fed him. He ran with them, not alone, merely following. An observer in life. This time, he leaves them a boy and returns in the morning one step closer to being a man."

"Great. There's a bar mitzvah for wolves."

"What's that?"

Darkly could tell that Buck was being truthful. She could read him like a book. He hadn't heard the word before.

"A bar mitzvah? Never mind."

Suddenly, Zachariah's head dipped below the grass, just as the orb of the sun dipped completely below the horizon. Neither popped back up.

"A deer, huh?"

"A deer. But, you're right. There are those of us who have hunted what we shouldn't. You saw me punish such a wolf. Sam returned to us after being away for many years. Bringing you and your friends to us was a way he sought forgiveness for his sins. There were those ready to give that forgiveness."

"Reverend MacIntyre?"

"No. He's all fire and brimstone. An eye for an eye and all that."

"On Sam's first moon run, he disappeared for a week. After returning to us, the town learned of a group of boy scouts massacred while camping almost one hundred miles away. Devoured."

"Why didn't you kill him then?"

"Would you have killed the child or given rehabilitation a shot?"

"He killed again?"

"In his late teens. A man, his pregnant wife, and their two children. We didn't see him again until you showed up. I carried out his sentence a little later than intended."

My God, thought Darkly. The young man she had seen in the campsite with her family. Could that have been Sam?

"So, why did Victoria--?" She cut her own self off. "Her first moon run?"

"That's right. She killed someone. An old trapper as isolated as we are, who could just have easily killed her if he wasn't half out of his mind. But, he was a human being nonetheless."

"Victoria killed Sam, I mean, tried to kill Sam, to show you all whose side she was on." Darkly's skills of deduction were putting her one step ahead of Buck.

"That she was one of us. Not like him." Buck confirmed Darkly's reasoning.

The bitter taste of coffee and death came back to Darkly. She had tasted her murder, but it had dissipated as Sam's body had healed. She was willing to bet that despite the derision that flew between Buck and Victoria, he was the one who demanded she be given another chance, even after Sam had shown an inability to change his nature.

Buck got up.

"You should head back to the hotel now. It's a big day tomorrow."

"Oh?"

Buck pulled off his cowboy boots.

"I'm going to take my clothes off now, Darkly."

"What?"

"I'm Zachariah's godfather. Since the trapper incident, all first moon runs are observed, from a distance, by the godfather of the child."

"To judge their true character."

"That's right."

Buck was now unbuttoning his shirt, and Darkly fought the instinct to follow suit and remove an article of her own clothing.

"You really should go now." Buck smiled.

"How do you know I won't make a run for it?"

"Go ahead. But remember, I can run a hell of a lot faster as a wolf. I will catch up. Do you have any silver bullets on you?"

Buck winked and turned away from her to finish undressing. Darkly began walking back to town, but couldn't resist a look back.

"What's tomorrow?"

Buck was already running down the hill. Darkly watched his naked human form disappear in tall grass.

Geraldine had taken a gamble in a couple of different ways. Would she be able to overpower Gus? She couldn't carry out the plan she had in mind while in wolf form, that was for sure. She had just over two hours before Zachariah began his first moon run. She could do this.

The crowbar was under her diner counter. She just needed to get Gus inside, make sure he was distracted, and then hit him over the head. One, two, three. Simple.

As they made their way down alongside the river, Geraldine explained to Gus that Darkly had fended off Buck's advances. He became angry, turned, and attacked her. Geraldine had shot and injured Buck, who ran off into the woods. Darkly was in her diner now, recovering. But, she'd lost a lot of blood.

Geraldine hoped she sounded sincere. Lying excited her, but she couldn't gauge how good she was at convincing others she was telling the truth.

When Gus ran into the empty diner, he found exactly what Geraldine had wanted him to find. In a booth, a pile vaguely the shape of a body was completely covered in a blanket.

"Oh, Christ. Darkly? Darkly?"

Gus only made it a few steps, when Geraldine raised the crow bar above his skull and threw it down like it was a mallet and she a strongman at a carnival. She hoped she hadn't killed him outright. That wouldn't do. No, that wouldn't do at all.

Now to retrieve the venison steaks she was defrosting in the sink. Suddenly, old Jasper stepped out of the Men's room, whistling. He shuffled up to Geraldine, carefully stepped over Gus's body and took a seat at the counter.

"Yep, I said they'd be staying for awhile. I think I'll have a hot cup of coffee, Geraldine."

"We're out of coffee, Jasper."

"What is this town coming to?"

CHAPTER SEVENTEEN

Buck knew he had gotten to Darkly. And she had gotten to him. He had always loved the boy he called his son as his own flesh and blood. They even looked alike in many ways. But, just as Trey would now start a family with Victoria, he felt the need to begin again.

Buck became the wolf in the tall grass, catching the scent of his godson ahead of him. But there was something else, the scent of deer. Buck could tell it was already dead. His nostrils were that keen.

Unlike the last run, Buck did not allow himself to lose his human identity entirely. It had taken many years of practice, but Buck had learned how to keep parts of his human mind active during a moon run. This was not always desired, as complete release was bliss, but this time he would hold on for Zachariah's sake. There was a job to do. He was here to supervise, to protect, to judge. This was a time for the sheriff of Wolf Woods as much as the animal in the night.

Buck tasted the droplet of blood on the grass. It wasn't deer. He knew that in an instant. The taste was unmistakable.

Wyatt was disowned. And Alpha no more. Geraldine had pleaded, cried, and torn out her hair for him. But he had killed one of their own who came in peace. What else could the sheriff, Wyatt and Buck's father, do? His position dictated he could not show favoritism. If he did, his, and then Buck's position, would become untenable.

Catharine was now under Luther's and Buck's protection. Buck would raise Wyatt's child that Catherine was carrying as his own. He had promised his father he would, in order to pay for the shame their family must now endure.

Word was spreading like a wild fire through the town. Catharine Darkly, or Stewart, as she now called herself, brought with her a cure. She had also brought with her a daughter, who had escaped. Young Buck had been entrusted with bringing the girl safely back to Wolf Woods. He caught her scent in the woods and then lost it at the edge of the great highway that had tamed a continent.

All he tasted was two bloody prints in the asphalt, where the child's feet had walked, the skin on her feet scraped away from miles of distance traveled.

Buck approached with caution. Zachariah was young, but he could still be dangerous, especially with a dead deer to protect. Buck emerged into a bed of pressed grass, where Zachariah was gnawing on Gus's leg. Gus was both blindfolded and gagged. Tied to his body, were cutlets of meat. Thankfully for Gus, he was unconscious.

Buck immediately tackled Zachariah. His godson was completely lost to a blood lust and fought back viciously. Buck was much stronger and bigger, and eventually pinned the younger wolf to the ground. Overwhelmed by his first moon run, Zachariah ran from the tall grass with his tail between his legs.

Gus was now in a bed in Doc Ross's home, where the doctor and Mrs. Ross could provide twenty-four-hour care. He was in a coma, and Doc wasn't sure he was coming out of it. Being this far from civilization, all he could hope for was that Gus's body might heal itself. Yet, Gus was no werewolf. Not yet.

In Buck's one and only jail cell, Geraldine sat on a cot. She was knitting a child's booties. She taunted Buck, who sat at his desk, staring into space.

"You said to separate them. I was giving you what you wanted. I eliminated your competition."

Buck ignored her.

"Are you going to banish me, Sheriff? Execute me? A silver bullet to my head like Sam?" Geraldine asked with complete calm.

Buck broke his silence. "Have you finally lost your mind?" Buck didn't look at Geraldine when he spoke to her.

Doc Ross and Reverend MacIntyre walked through the door. Geraldine turned her attention to them.

"Did you know they're Mounties sent here to flush us out? Then kill us. You know how I know? The boots always give them away. Every couple of years, one will pass through town, stop in at my diner, ask what's been going on. Same as last time you asked me, Constable. Nothing. So goes the life of a small town that isn't even on the map."

"If you knew what they were, why didn't you say something to me sooner, Geraldine?" asked Buck.

Geraldine said nothing in return.

"Is this true, Sheriff?" asked Reverend MacIntyre.

Buck wasn't in the mood to humor anyone. "That we're not on the map?"

Geraldine irritated Buck by holding up the booties, pretending to examine her work.

Buck finally answered the Reverend. "They are Mounties, and no, they aren't here to hunt us."

"How can you be so sure? Perhaps being in such a hurry to impress the girl, you forgot to interrogate her?" Score another point for Geraldine.

Buck knew what Geraldine was doing here. She was trying to instill doubt in the minds of Doc Ross and the Reverend. There wasn't much Buck could do against her if she had their support.

"How is he, Doc?" Buck asked.

Doc just shook his head.

"That's how you interrogate someone, isn't it, Geraldine? You feed them to the Doc's kin." Buck knew that thought would get Doc back on his side.

Geraldine was about to drop a bomb.

"Have you taken a close look at her yet, Buck? I mean a really close look at her. Or does she not let you get that close? She's Catharine's daughter."

The Reverend coughed.

"Catharine who?" Doc Ross asked.

"Catharine Stewart," Geraldine answered, cool as a salamander. "Are there any other Catharine's you know, Doc? You remember her maiden name, Darkly. A good Scottish name that. Your children were too old to wear those instruments of torture, Doc. But, I'll never forget what Heaven's Rain looks like. Victoria cried every minute she wasn't asleep from the exhaustion that "the cure" brought her. Thank God she's too young to remember it. The pain will become bearable in time, Catharine told us. "It may even become comforting, as it has for my own daughter," she said. Oh, it prevented the transformations, but how many went mad because of it? How many became outcasts in their own homes? There's no doubt it affected my daughter's disposition. No doubt."

The remembrance of horrors past forced Reverend MacIntyre to take a seat. "I remember the screams," he said.

"Hadn't we suffered enough, Reverend? All those years in the wilderness?"

Geraldine would play the Reverend like a fiddle, the soppy old fool. She'd play them all.

"Stop it, Geraldine," Buck spit into the air.

Buck knew better than to debate the issue. He always saw Geraldine's attacks coming and was always powerless to fight them. The guilt he felt for his brother's actions that left two women without a husband and two daughters without a father, it would always give Geraldine the upper hand.

The Reverend rocked in his chair, clutching his temples. "Suffer the little children."

"Let's not bring this up again. The cure was abandoned by everyone," Buck reminded them. "End of story."

"Except for one, Buck. She kept taking the cure on her own. God knows how she did it, but she did. Imagine what her mental state must be like now? Homicidal?"

Buck threw the mug he kept on his desk hard against the bars of Geraldine's cell.

"Enough!"

The mug shattered into dozens of pieces. Doc stepped between Buck and Geraldine, placing a fatherly hand of restraint on Buck's shoulder.

Geraldine picked a thin shard of the mug out of her cheek. A pinprick of blood oozed forth.

"She bears the scars of torture, Buck. Willingly. Your future mate is touched, Sheriff."

Buck, Doc, and the Reverend continued on with their discussion in Doc's office. The Reverend was near hysterics.

"We all know what happened the last time our kind put our faith in the government's forces. Now one of our own is a collaborator? This could be the end of us. No one to carry on the quest for redemption."

Buck tried to be the voice of reason, but this was a debate that ran red with the blood of countless centuries.

"That was a long time ago. We don't have a collaborator infiltrating our ranks. You see, this is exactly what Geraldine wants us to do. Panic."

So, Darkly is the girl who left those bloody footprints on the highway seventeen years before, thought Buck.

"I don't believe she has knowledge of what she is. She merely needs to be shown, and she will embrace it," Buck hoped out loud.

"What do we do about the others?" Doc asked.

"Just what we planned to do all along. We throw them a party."

Then, the Reverend asked what the other two were afraid to bring up.

"What about Catharine?"

"What about her?" Buck asked rhetorically to end the discussion.

CHAPTER EIGHTEEN

Calmer minds prevailed. But not right away. Catharine caught a glimpse of her daughter's eyes as she was dragged out of the RV. Wyatt's jaws were locked over one of her ankles, and her head slammed against the metal grating on the steps leading to the outside. It ripped at her cheeks, further igniting her rage.

She saw the wolves standing over Jack's broken body, his wolf head separated from his wolf body. They were whimpering. Wyatt had killed one of their own, and the rest were now unsure of what to do. They were mere teenagers following Wyatt, supposed to do whatever he commanded. He would, after all, inherit the Alpha position. As Catharine watched her husband's body return to human, she became wolf.

Buck had done as his father ordered. He understood that sometimes killing an outsider would help his own kind survive. But that didn't make it any more palatable. The decision was never taken lightly, and Buck's father had supported the old ways throughout his days as sheriff. He had kept their population hidden, as much to protect the outside world as themselves. It was his sons, Wyatt and Buck, who would bring in the new age, once Wyatt was ready and wise enough to challenge him. But that day was not today. And after this night's course of events, it would never likely come.

Luther called off the hunt. Catharine was taken to the doctor. Her wounds would heal. What else could they do? Werewolves were the next best thing to immortal. No disease or mere injury could take them while they were alive. Only silver, fire, or beheading could cut a long life short. Old age brought a quiet death. One would slip out of town near the end, find a secluded spot at sunset, and fall asleep under a bright moon. The body would be retrieved before it was eaten by scavengers.

Jack was dead. That could easily have been avoided. Wyatt went for his neck *after* he had turned. There was no denying he was a werewolf. Luther had hoped Wyatt would grow out of his propensity for acting rashly and that more responsibility would nurture restraint. It had not. Now, Wyatt must be killed or banished.

Luther anticipated how this would go. Wyatt would attack his father. He would make his bid before the town council could pass judgment on him. Successful, Wyatt would gather his army of youths to him, and all dissenters would be punished.

Luther could not allow the town to fall into the hands of his eldest son. It would be their ruin. He must prepare his young son, Buck, for the war ahead. Buck was only twenty, not ready for the responsibility. He hadn't even taken a proper mate. Wyatt had taken Geraldine, taken her from Buck, which was his right to do. He was the Alpha apparent. Buck must be made ready.

Luther began preparing Buck for the fight that would come in weeks, not months. Wyatt was not stupid. He would not attack immediately after a display of his own weakness. He would make himself scarce and not act until the town faced its next threat, and his father's impotent response demanded new leadership. Luther raised Buck's status by making Catharine, and her unborn child—Wyatt's unborn child, Buck's responsibility.

Catharine had turned fully and defended herself against Wyatt. It had been decades since the play fighting of her youth. She was out of shape and overwhelmed with grief for her husband. She got in a couple good bites, as Wyatt's yelps attested to. But, he did pin her. He straddled her, forcing her to submit, with his jaws in the back of her neck. Wyatt mounted Catharine, and she howled in sorrow.

Luther and Buck arrived at the RV to find Wyatt and his gang of thugs standing over Jack's body. Someone had retrieved a blanket from the RV and thrown it over Catharine, who was huddled under a tree in shock. Luther ordered Buck to take Catharine to Doc Ross. Buck lifted the unresponsive woman into his arms.

"Where were you, little brother? I didn't give you permission to leave."

Buck didn't answer Wyatt. He walked off with Catharine and left his brother to Luther.

"Go home," said Luther.

Wyatt and the other young men turned to go.

"Not you," said Luther to Wyatt. "You're going to bury this wolf. The wolf you murdered."

Luther said this loud enough for all of Wyatt's followers to hear.

"Murdered? I was under your orders. You told me to kill him."

"I told you to kill a man, not murder a werewolf and rape his wife."

Wyatt thought carefully about his response.

"You raised an Alpha to act in the best interests of this town. We need more women of breeding age. Thanks to me, we have one more. With a ready-made child, if I did my job well."

"I raised two Alphas."

Luther turned to follow Buck back to town.

Wyatt understood what his father had said all too well.

Wyatt made his move just after the birth of his son. The son that was taken away from him. Trey had his mother's black hair. He was a Darkly.

Wyatt had always hated that family. Claiming their right to sit in judgment over the rest of them simply because they could trace their family back to the only surviving wilderness child of Nebuchadnezzar. They viewed themselves as the only true werewolves. Everyone else was just a walking STD.

Catharine escaping Wolf Woods devastated her parents. Her mother died of a broken heart, and her father, Old Man Darkly, stepped down as magistrate the day after his wife died, walked out into the woods and was never seen again. No body was retrieved. Wyatt knew the reason for that. He'd followed the old man out into the woods, killed him, and then ate him. That was the greatest show of disrespect one werewolf could show another. Now who was lord of the realm?

There would be no return of the Darkly family. Once Wyatt had taken care of Luther, he would come for Catharine. And Trey—never mind that he was half Wyatt. He wouldn't kill his turncoat wife. He'd teach her a lesson. Maybe bite off an arm. A finger might grow back. But a whole arm?

The day came when Luther let a trucker go. The man was hauling canned goods. He'd stumbled along the little town after a couple unfortunate wrong turns. Over a bowl of oatmeal at The Moon River Diner, he told Luther his sad tale. He was a father of five, newly a widower, and now the only bread winner. Luther had lost Buck's mother in childbirth. The child would have been a sister to Buck and Wyatt. But neither she nor Luther's wife survived.

Luther took pity on the trucker and let him go. When Wyatt caught up with the trucker, killed the man, and brought back two years' worth of food with him, Luther was out and Wyatt in.

Wyatt passed out silver bullets to his posse, and they descended on the sheriff, charging him with dereliction of duty. Luther informed his oldest son he would have to shoot him with one of those bullets before he stepped foot in his own jail cell. So, that's just what Wyatt did. Then, he and his wolves showed up at Buck's door.

Catharine's mental state was compromised. Months of fighting nature would do that to you. But, even in this state, she could tell Buck was not bluffing. And she suddenly wanted her son to live. Very much so.

She let go.

Buck put down the gun and nodded at Geraldine.

"We bring Wyatt down, and the rest will scatter," said Buck.

Now three wolves faced the onslaught together, as the door gave way, and the table was thrown aside like a piece of cardboard.

And just as Buck had banked on, the mother wolf guarding her young, who slept soundly without fear, attacked the young wolves loyal to Wyatt with a ferocity they were not prepared for. Wyatt and Catharine soon focused solely on one another, as Geraldine and Buck held the less experienced fighters at bay.

Catharine took revenge for both her husband and herself. She suffered puncture wounds to her jaw, chest and hindquarters. But, in the end, her jaws found their way to Wyatt's trachea, where they did not let go. And despite the hatred that transcended her human condition, Catharine knew as a wolf, that Wyatt must slink away beaten, for his followers to abandon the cause and him.

Wyatt was last seen limping up the ridge. Alone.

CHAPTER NINETEEN

Peter let go of the grip he had on Shane's curly hair, kissed his neck, and then rolled over to spread out across the sheets exhausted. He had been holding that in for awhile. He and Shane had found each other attractive early on. They were both gay, fit, good-looking and decent guys. Both were in committed, happy relationships, and respected that.

"I mean, my God," Shane wittily remarked, "It's not like we're actresses. We don't have to fuck our co-star."

But, now, looking across the room at the 1950s suit that had been delivered to his room for what was described to him as his courting session, Peter felt that the couple hours he and Shane shared together this morning could end up being the last opportunity in his life to throw caution to the wind.

Victoria escorted Serena to the party.

"If you try to run, I'll turn into a wolf and bring you back in pieces," Victoria said frankly.

Serena didn't reply, and Victoria realized she might have come on a little strong.

"Your dress looks nice."

The dress was, in fact, hideous. It was a white cotton dress with mini black umbrellas printed all over it. White was being generous. It was actually more a gray, due to the discoloring of age. Serena had no choice but to put it on, as Victoria hovered over her in threatening fashion.

"You're going to a party. People should smile at parties."

Serena responded by popping another pill.

"What are those?"

"Supplements," Serena answered.

"Well, I'd make them last. We don't have a 'supplement' shop."

Serena found her backbone briefly.

"If I'm forced to become one of you people, the first thing I'm doing is this—"

Serena grabbed her own arm, bit into it, and pretended to shake the arm and growl.

Victoria gave Serena her space the rest of the way to the church.

Gus was drifting in and out of semi-consciousness. There was no escape Darkly could make while he was in this state. A Mountie did not abandon another Mountie. Buck knew this, so she was allowed to wander freely in town. Still, as a precaution, the two working telephones were put under armed guard in case she decided to alert her superiors.

Mrs. Ross was a caring nurse. She doted on Gus, repositioning him on the hour to prevent bedsores, and even bathing him. Dealing with such dead weight could not have been an easy task. She never complained, and she insisted on feeding Darkly at mealtimes.

Seeing as Gus's condition did not appear to be taking a dramatic turn in either direction, Darkly did not feel guilty being dragged away to this little party the town had organized. She and the other visitors were the guests of honor after all, and Buck had promised to dispel the notion that his people were only monsters.

She would humor the town's notions, not rock the boat. When Gus was ready, he, Darkly, and the rest of the group would escape. Then she would come back in force and arrest the lot of them. If Geraldine resisted that arrest, she'd shoot her. With a silver bullet. Buck too, if she had to.

The question remained, what was she going to wear to the dance?

Buck delivered Carter, Marvin, Shane, Peter, and Jake to the party in the bed of his pick-up truck. Ed was in the front seat with Buck. He was carrying a small bouquet of wild flowers and wearing a bow tie.

"Tie that tie yourself, Ed?" Buck asked.

"Of course I did. Who else would have tied it?"

They arrived at the church hall, and Ed stood watch like the guard of a chain gang over the men they were transporting. It made for quite the sight. Five men in ill-fitting suits followed by a giant carrying posies.

Inside, it was evident the town had splurged. Corned beef sandwiches, cakes of every size, homemade whisky punch, streamers, and a couple of fiddle players in the corner leading children under twelve in a square dance. This was a get-together with a very serious purpose, but also the opportunity for a community to blow off steam. The guns were put away and replaced with laughter and good will.

Carter came from a wealthy family, which attracted hangers-on. Sex came easy, but not once had he met a woman who would take him without the money. Then again, to be fair, he wasn't much more than a shadow of his father's accomplishments. He had never tried to find out who he was, so why should anyone else bother? He was a piggy bank: empty save for the coins rattling around inside.

Mary sat in a chair off to the side of a group of young women who were stealing looks at the visitors and comparing notes.

Carter wasn't sure what it was about Mary that caught his interest in an instant. Maybe it was the shape of her nose or mouth. Maybe it was simply the fact that she looked away when others gawked. When she finally did look their way, she looked at him. Not Jake or Marvin, not one of the handsome actors; she looked at him. And in her eyes he saw the opposite of empty.

As Carter and Mary stared at each other, Darkly descended on the party and drew the attention of more than just Buck in the little black number she borrowed from Mrs. Ross. It smelled a little of moth balls, but the 1940s retro-chic dress with a high Chinese collar was a knock-out.

Buck had laid claim to Darkly in the town council meeting. Now, it was time to make clear his intentions to everyone else. He walked up to Darkly and placed his hand on the small of her back.

Darkly recognized what the gesture meant.

"I see," she said, staring a hole through Buck until he blinked.

"There's someone I'd like you to meet," said Buck, changing the unspoken subject.

"Your mother?"

"My mother's dead. Just like my father."

Darkly was chastened. "I'm very sorry."

Carter couldn't believe he was about to march right up and talk to the woman in the corner. This ridiculous invite to settle down in Wolf Woods or die by the jaws of a wolf didn't inspire one to cross a bridge to friendship and perhaps something more. But that was exactly what his feet seemed intent on doing.

Then Buck got in the way. He guided Darkly over to the corner and introduced her to Mary. At least Carter knew her name now.

"It's nice to meet you," Mary said in a faint voice.

Mary waited for Darkly to reply, but Darkly was mesmerized by the spiderweb of blue veins that crisscrossed Mary's chest above the neckline of her modest dress. The lines were fainter than Darkly's, submerged under the skin, but extensive in their reach. Mary followed Darkly's gaze and pulled a shawl around herself.

"It's nice to meet you too, Mary," Darkly said far too late.

Mary got up with some difficulty and excused herself. She reached behind her and grabbed two wooden canes hanging on the back of the chair. She used both canes to hobble past Carter and his cast and crew, who were holding plates onto which the older women of the church were piling the food they'd prepared. Carter turned to watch Mary leave the church basement. Buck took note of this. One more match down. That was easy, and he had to admit, a little unexpected.

"Why did you introduce me to her?" asked Darkly.

At that moment, one of the fiddle players called the adults to the floor to dance. Buck watched in amusement, as the old ladies who had handed the men food now took it away and led them each to the women standing on the other side of the room, ordering them to dance. Awkwardly and wary of the consequences of disobedience, they did as they were told. Clearly, the women were expecting to be led in a waltz. What resulted was much fidgeting of placement of hands and a general shuffling of feet under the spell of no particular rhythm.

Buck turned to take Darkly's hand, with the intent of leading her to the dance floor.

"I thought you might have a few things in common."

Darkly ignored the gesture and sat down in Mary's vacated seat.

"I see what you mean. Mary and I are both wallflowers."

While this drama was wrapping up, another was blooming. When Victoria arrived with Serena, she marched her right up to Ed and handed her off.

"Here she is," Victoria told Ed. "Good luck," she said to Serena in parting.

Serena looked up at Ed, and he down at her. Not knowing what to do, Ed handed Serena the flowers and went out to sit in Buck's truck. He left Serena standing there, in shock, staring at a cluster of ragweed and dandelions tied together with string and wishing this nightmare would come to an end.

Carter and his men were passed around the room. When Buck felt they had been tortured enough, he called a halt to the music and addressed the whole room.

"It's nice to see we haven't forgotten how to hold a dance."

Darkly spotted Serena across the room and went to her. Serena just stared at the floor, while Buck continued.

"Seventeen years ago, we thought we had found a way to fit in with the outside world. One of our own left us and then returned with the promise of a cure."

Buck looked directly at Darkly.

"It didn't quite turn out that way. She and her husband were good people."

Dissent rose up from the party-goers, and Buck raised his hands to halt it.

"No, they were. Their intentions were honorable, but what had worked on their own child," Buck paused here to let what he was saying sink in with Darkly, "drove our children to madness or left them plagued with recurring ailments. Too few recovered, and too many died."

Darkly saw the flash of a woman's hands working the metal, crafting the necklace she herself wore, hidden under her dress. She reached up to touch its outline through the material.

"So we renewed our hopes for another way out of hiding. There is always hope."

This was Buck the politician speaking, and he connected individually with the people he led: a nod to one old farmer, a pat on the head for a grandson, a smile for a mother. Buck's eyes next met those of Victoria and Trey.

"And though we continue on, building new families, there are no longer enough of us to sustain a community."

Buck paused. The people nodded their heads in acknowledgment of the stark reality.

"Some of our young people volunteered to leave and find their mates in the outside world. We do not know if we will see them again. If they are successful, then our kind will spread, and, eventually, the secret will be so common, it will no longer be a secret."

Buck walked up to Carter and spoke to him, man to man.

"So we offer you a bargain. All of you. Choose your wife here from among us. Mate. And when your first child is the age of one, we will let you go. You will return to your homes with your new families, and your children will change the world."

"Is he saying you become a werewolf by fucking one of them?" Shane whispered to Peter.

"Yes," replied Peter. "What planet have you been visiting the past twenty-four hours?"

CHAPTER TWENTY

Darkly returned to Gus's side and took over his care from Mrs. Ross so that she could go to the party and dance with her husband. Darkly had to remind herself of the danger even *she* faced of succumbing to Stockholm syndrome. A good-looking sheriff who wanted her doggy style and a doctor's wife who reminded her of Mrs. Claus aside, these people, this whole town, was guilty of kidnapping and of threatening with bodily harm.

Darkly considered Mary. Buck knew she had the same mark as Mary. He had seen it on her, or someone else had and reported it to him. Had Mary worn a necklace fashioned by her biological mother? To prevent her from turning into a werewolf? And had that necklace left her a cripple? Did that mean Darkly was a werewolf? No, that couldn't be. There was nothing wrong with her. She had worn the necklace for longer than she could remember. No deformities.

She heard the front door open downstairs.

"Darkly?" It was Buck's voice.

What if she didn't answer?

"May I come up?"

Would he think she escaped? No, he'd figured her out. He knew it was her duty to escape, but also that she'd find a way to get everyone else out with her. Yet, Buck was a man, and men gave a lot of credence to their charm. He would try to convince her she was right where she belonged. With him.

Darkly also knew that if Buck thought she was softening to the idea, he would be easier to deceive when the time came.

"Yes. I'm up here."

Buck appeared a few minutes later. He carried two plates. One of sandwiches and one of cake.

"I noticed you didn't eat anything."

Buck placed the plates on a dresser and looked down on Gus.

"How's he doing?" asked Buck.

There was genuine regret in his voice.

"He still hasn't regained consciousness," replied Darkly.

"If he doesn't make it, Geraldine will face a trial. You have my word on that."

"If he doesn't make it? So, if Gus heals entirely, no harm done? If he wakes up but can't use his legs ever again, does she get community service?"

"You should know that Geraldine saved your mother's life."

Buck went on to relate the events that took place from the time when Darkly was hidden in the RV to well past the time she was transported across the country.

"Okay, hold on, cowboy," Darkly said pacing the room. "If I'm one of you, why hasn't this necklace made me a cripple?"

"Are you telling me it's not uncomfortable in the least?" Buck replied.

Darkly didn't answer the questioning. She didn't have to do anything. She was the only law that mattered here now.

"Trey. Your brother. He wasn't thrilled about wearing the necklace, but he came away unharmed."

Darkly didn't try to hide the rolling of her eyes.

"He is your brother."

"You turn yourself in to me at the nearest RCMP post, and I will happily take a genetic test."

Buck ignored the suggestion.

"Your mother put an end to Trey's treatment when she saw what it was doing to the other children. I didn't want her to. I was young and suggested we make a run for it. We'd take Trey back to Portland and live a quiet life. But your mother insisted she stay to make amends for the damage she'd done to the people of Wolf Woods. That was the kind of woman she was, Darkly."

"And don't tell me, for her penance, the good werewolves of Wolf Woods chased her down and ate her."

Darkly still wasn't buying the morbid fairy tale.

"No, Darkly, that's not what happened at all. I can take you to see her, to see your mother, if you like."

At that moment, Gus regained consciousness.

Darkly and Buck set out on the two-day trek. They began on the river, down which they would paddle for half a day, then hike for another day and a half to reach Catharine's home.

Catharine, Buck explained, had not been banished by the town. She banished herself. She had spent the whole of her adult life looking for a cure for lupinism, only to produce an outcome worthy of the Nazi doctor, Mengele. She could not face the parents whose children would grow up to be lunatics and cripples. She had failed to save her husband, her daughter, and the children of Wolf Woods. She wanted to live a self-enforced isolation, where she would cause no harm to anyone ever again.

Darkly had decided to embrace the explanations until they were disproved. She could not dispel what she had witnessed in the diner. So, she found herself paddling into the wilderness with a redneck sheriff in search of her mother, a werewolf, whom she had not seen in almost two decades and could barely remember other than in flashes of daydreams.

Darkly stopped paddling. Not because her arms were tired, but because something didn't make sense.

"Why Trey and me? Why are we spared?"

She felt her moon pendant, reminding herself that the necklace she never took off was still there.

Buck stopped paddling.

"Well, this is as good a time as any for a break," he said, lifting an oar out of the water and into the canoe. "Darkly Stewart, you are a descendant of the first werewolf."

"You have an answer for everything. That's what we call a bullshit artist in the outside world."

"It's true, Darkly. Not the bullshit bit. The first werewolf part. When Nebudchanezzar was exiled to the wilderness, he mated with wolves while he was in wolf form himself. The Darklys, your mother's clan, are direct descendants of those children."

"How does that make me special?"

"We don't know. The Reverend says because God forgave Nebudchanezzar and lifted his curse, and the Darklys are closer to him by blood."

"Maybe we're a little closer to salvation?"

"Who knows, Darkly?"

Darkly lifted the pendant off her skin.

"And if I remove the necklace, I will turn?"

"I don't know that either."

Darkly let the pendant fall back onto its resting place.

"It could be you've worn that thing so long, you really have found salvation."

Buck picked up his oar and slid it back into the water.

"So the rest of you are just the product of peasants raped by a werewolf? And I'm your queen?"

Buck laughed.

"Something like that."

Darkly slid her oar back into the water, and both began to paddle again. But, once again, Darkly stopped.

"Oh my God. Trey and Victoria are half brother and sister. And you're letting them—"

Buck didn't miss a beat in rowing when he interrupted Darkly.

"No, I'm not and, no, they're not."

"According to you, your brother raped my mother," Darkly said, begging to differ most emphatically.

"And I made him pay for that. But, your brother is your full brother. Wyatt is not his father. Although, only a few people know that. With werewolves, Darkly," Buck went on to explain, "the Alpha remains Alpha until he is challenged by the son who is to become Alpha or dies childless. With Wyatt banished, his son becomes the Alpha-to-be, and I became the caretaker until he is ready to assume his responsibility. If the whole town knew Trey was not of my blood, not Wyatt's son, the whole system would be thrown into chaos, and the position of Alpha would be up for grabs."

"Ah, you mean democracy," Darkly stabbed Buck with her wit.

"No, Darkly. I mean many wolves dead and families torn apart as an entire community questions where their loyalties lie."

Darkly and Buck paddled in silence the rest of the way. Upon reaching an outcrop of rock early in the afternoon, Buck directed the canoe to a small inlet in the river.

They pulled the canoe fully up onto the river bank, grabbed their backpacks, and began hiking up a mountainside. Darkly allowed herself to think of her dad, William, the man who raised her. She had not been gone long enough for him to begin worrying. But, if he knew where she was, surely a little bit of him would be envious of the adventure she was undertaking into the bush, with only the stars above her and virgin ground below.

In Wolf Woods, Geraldine had been let out to return to her daughter and diner. Gus, having regained consciousness, left her off-the-hook for the most part. Such was the law in a small town where the labors of even one person are sorely missed.

When it came to lunch, she really was the town cafeteria. The townsfolk all had their gardens and knew how to can their vegetables for winter, but it was Geraldine's place where they connected over her biscuits and rabbit stew. This was where people pretended they were like everyone else on the planet.

Just like in a restaurant in New York City, Geraldine would present the bill at the end of the meal. Only, instead of numbers, a small chalkboard slate would list ingredients requested in lieu of monetary payment. Customers would return later that day or the next day with a basket of peppers or eggs or a leg of lamb.

Last year, Martha Bowie dug up a gallon jug filled with salt, planted in her back garden by her grandmother a decade before for safe keeping. Martha ate at the diner free for a month.

In the diner tonight, while Darkly was away searching for answers and Gus was lying in bed wondering if he'd ever be able to walk again, the film cast and crew were paired off in booths and at tables, where they were expected to get to know better the young women they selected.

Selected is a gross exaggeration. Reverend MacIntyre, Doc Ross, and Buck had consulted on where there seemed to be the most potential for happy unions and then instructed the chosen girls to be present for their first date tonight at The Moon River Diner.

Geraldine, Victoria, and Trey had done the place up nice. Every other light bulb had been removed from the ceiling to create mood lighting. Candles had been placed at all of the tables, and curtains almost forgotten in a box in the attic had been fashioned into table cloths. Geraldine was serving chicken with mushroom sauce. There seemed to always be plenty of chicken available.

In one booth, Marvin and Jake, the youngest of the men, were listening to twins go on and on about their Uncle Buck's son, Trey. It was pretty clear Marjorie and Doreen Robertson were looking for replacements for that crush, and they'd both decided Marvin and Jake fit the bill. Though, they repeatedly got Marvin and Jake's names confused. Whereas, Marvin and Jake never called either twin by anything but their correct name. Fear has a way of concentrating one's concentration.

In another booth, Peter was trying to ascertain if his match, a blonde beauty queen type with fluffed up hair from another era, had read a book published since 1963.

Shane was having to constantly shift his feet, while the mousy girl across from him dipped lower and lower in her chair trying to reach him with hers.

Behind Shane, Serena sat across from a twelve-year-old girl named Lily, who sat calmly filing her long nails. Lily was Ed's daughter.

"You're very pretty," said Lily.

It wasn't said as a compliment, but as a genuine observation.

"Thank you," replied Serena.

"Are you going to be my new mother?"

"I..." Serena had no clue how to reply to that.

"My father likes you, but says I'm a better judge of what he needs."

"That's a lot of responsibility for you."

"I'm used to it."

"What happened to your mother?" Serena asked, genuinely curious.

"She's dead."

Serena was sorry she asked, because now all sorts of horror stories about how that death came about were running through her head.

"My father thinks you're too skinny, and that you don't smile. He says you'd probably make a bad mother."

"Does your father always judge people before he gets to know them?"

"I guess."

"Well, I think I'd make a very good mother. I love kids. But, Lily, I have a life somewhere else I really want to get back to. I have a mother who misses me as much as I bet you miss your mother."

Great, thought Serena, she's now explaining through rationalization to a precocious little girl why she should let her go home.

"I never knew my mother. She died giving birth to me. I was too big."

Lily stood up.

"See? I'm a lot taller than most girls my age."

It was true. At twelve, Lily was already a few inches beyond five feet.

"Well, Lily," Serena tread carefully, "It's not your fault your mother died. She wanted you."

"It's my fault," replied Lily with no sense sorrow. "My father said so."

"Your father said that to you?"

"Yep."

Serena reached out to Lily.

"Oh, sweetheart, no. That's not true."

Geraldine had appeared at their table to clear Lily's plate away. Serena still hadn't touched hers. Geraldine joined in on the debate.

"No, it's true. Doc Ross could confirm it. Lily was too big for Beatrice's birth canal. So, ice cream or chocolate cake?"

Geraldine elongated the word chocolate for Lily's sake.

"What is wrong with you?" Serena responded, dumbfounded. Geraldine took Serena's untouched plate and returned to the kitchen without acknowledging the indignation.

Then there was Carter. Carter was the only one of the visitors looking forward to tonight. He was told Mary would join him at six o'clock for supper. Her father dropped her off outside the diner at ten minutes past. With her two canes, she made her way the dozen feet to the diner's door, where Trey, who was bussing that night, got the door for her and pointed her in Carter's direction.

Mary Ross was a relation of the Doc's. Her mind had survived the cure, but her body hadn't. She would never walk without canes again. As a human, anyway.

Carter was no more thrilled with being held prisoner by monsters than the rest of the group. They seemed to be relatively benign monsters. Although, no one had satisfactorily explained what happened to Gus. Yet, Carter couldn't deny the fact that when looking into Mary's eyes, he saw a soul of beauty, intelligence, and grace shaped by a chosen response to suffering that did not embrace self-pity. He saw a strength he did not have but wished to possess.

Carter got up to help Mary to her seat. She stopped and flicked her hand.

"Thank you. I can sit down myself."

Mary took a seat and slid her canes under the table. Carter noticed her hands were affected too, by the way she fumbled with her knife to get to the napkin underneath and how she draped it over her lap.

"Do you eat here often?" Carter asked, nervously.

"I eat at home."

"Of course."

"I..." They both spoke at once.

"Sorry," conceded Carter. "You first."

"I'm not sure why I'm here."

"To eat?" Carter lightened the mood.

Mary smiled in a way that led Carter to believe she was out of practice.

"I wish you could have seen me first as something else. I'm not as…" she searched for the right word, "…broken when I'm a wolf."

"I think you're perfect just the way you are. Should we order?"

Across the river, a dozen werewolves circled the abandoned RVs and vehicle that once made up the film's circus before turning their attention to the overlook and the house lights twinkling below.

The look in Wyatt's eyes had gone from devil-may-care to crazy. His body was still lean and wiry, though his hair was now pure white.

"It's been too long, little brother."

CHAPTER TWENTY-ONE

Darkly and Buck ate fish over a fire that night. Buck had the sense to drag a line behind the canoe on their journey. They lost the light and were out the moment their heads hit the ground. They were both tired from the river, and Darkly had to admit she felt safer inside a tent with Buck than on her own. Well, that was as it should be. He knew this territory. She didn't.

Darkly woke in the middle of the night and turned to see Buck was missing. She opened the tent flap and looked up at the sky. It was a clear night, and she noticed how the moon's light caught her pendant.

"Buck?" Darkly called out to him.

There was no answer.

She listened to the babble of the nearby stream. Was he taking care of business? She looked at the moon again. Or was he taking care of other *business*? Darkly remembered how Buck had looked at Carter in the diner. She wasn't banking that Buck the wolf would deal with her any differently.

She tied the tent flaps together tightly. Like that would stop a wolf. Her adrenaline was pumping now. She wouldn't be able to sleep. Her mind was racing. What if this was the plan all along? Was this some sort of test? Would Darkly be confronted by a type of danger that would finally make her rip off the moon pendant and become what God intended her to be?

Darkly laid awake thinking every sound outside the tent was made for her benefit.

Morning found Darkly groggy. She woke to the sound of a crackling fire. At least she knew Buck was back. She emerged from the tent and found a small pot on the coals of the fire. It contained water with roots floating in it. Tea? She poured some into a cup and sipped. She was expecting a bitter experience and got something entirely different. A bit earthy, but it seemed to perk her up.

Where was Buck? She decided to make her way down to the stream. Maybe he was getting more water. She walked across the slope of the heavily wooded mountainside, occasionally slipping, then climbing, a few paces to remain on a straight path. Darkly arrived at the carved out track that rushed water down to the valley below to join the river that ran through Wolf Woods.

She found Buck. He was washing in the stream, rinsing clumps of dirt out of his hair in frantic motions. In fact, all of his body was covered in dirt. He was also naked.

"Did you bring my clothes?" Buck yelled to her through the water he was pouring over his hair and face.

Darkly, surprised, turned around. This was not something she found easy to do. What's more, she sensed Buck knew she was drawn to him.

"Sorry," she half spoke, half whispered.

"I thought you'd be asleep for a while longer. I thought I had time to get dressed."

"I understand. Why are you so dirty?"

"I traveled pretty far last night. I picked up the scent of a wolf pack. It's a little hard, in that state, not to follow them. We're territorial creatures."

"I'll just go get your clothes."

"I appreciate it."

Buck had to admit to himself, he was loosening up thanks to Darkly.

A fully clothed Buck and Darkly sat around the fire finishing their tea.

"What is this root?" Darkly asked.

"You know, I don't really know. I dug it up and ate it once as a wolf, so I know it's not poisonous. As a man, I like it better in tea."

Darkly put her tea down. She didn't think she would end up finishing it.

"You said you smelled a wolf pack last night. How do they react to you?"

"They can tell I'm different in some way. That I don't belong. So, they just avoid me. There's rarely a confrontation between us and them."

"Different in what way?"

"The best way I can describe it is, say you meet someone from a different country who doesn't speak any English. You both look similar, but there is definitely a block to communicating."

"Did you chase them off?"

"No, they made their way through here a few days ago. I was following their residual scent."

Buck downed the rest of his tea.

"I recognized my brother's scent actually. We should make a move."

Buck pulled one of the tent stakes out of the ground.

"Wait," Darkly said. "Wyatt? You smelled the man who killed my father?"

"I've caught his scent before this far out. He grew up hunting in these woods. I expect him to return from time to time."

Buck finished pulling the stakes out of the ground and was now rolling up the tent.

"The strange thing is, he's always alone. This time, I smelled other wolves with him."

"What does that mean?"

"I guess that he's lonely. Anyway, the scent was heading away from Wolf Woods. That's all I care about."

Darkly and Buck lifted their packs over their shoulders and resumed their trek up the slope.

Wyatt had returned to his old hunting grounds six or seven times since he was betrayed by his family. He had picked up his brother's scent a few times too, while Buck patrolled his precious town. The town that should be Wyatt's.

Thanks to Buck, Wyatt had not seen his and Geraldine's child born. And it was thanks to Buck, that a fucking Darkly still lived. Now, Wyatt was building his own clan. He'd show this town what bad things could happen when their sheriff neglected his duties.

Wyatt had been clever in making his way here with his clan. They'd spent a week traveling in the opposite direction, working their way around two mountains to double back to the town. If Buck ever picked up his scent, he would think his brother was merely passing through the fringes of his territory.

Wyatt's spies had told him that his brother was a two-day hike from Wolf Woods. A lot of damage could be done in two days. He wouldn't kill Trey. No, he'd recruit him and train him to kill the man who raised him. Only then would Wyatt kill his son.

Or maybe he'd wait until his other son, Roland, was old enough, and make Trey the boy's first kill. A rite of passage. Then, hand him Victoria as the prize. Not as a wife, just a plaything. Wyatt had learned that his daughter was now married to his son, her half-brother. Wolf Woods under Buck's leadership had become so desperate, they'd resorted to inbreeding.

"Wolf Woods," Wyatt proclaimed to the wind, "your favorite son returns."

"Are we going down there today, babe?" Wyatt's wife, Angie, asked.

Angie had been Wyatt's mate for the past fourteen years. She was just over half his age, and she'd given him Roland, who had just turned thirteen.

"Tomorrow. I want Buck to realize he was just a few hours too late. Until then, tell the rest we stay hidden. Tell Roland not to go wandering off."

Wyatt looked at Angie's clothes. She was wearing a tight-fitting outfit she'd taken from Serena's RV. They were all wearing the cast's clothes.

"Damn, Mama Wolf, you like fine!"

"I want to look my best when I meet your family."

"Oh, they are going to love you."

Serena had agreed, for Lily's sake, to spend some time at her home. The actress had grown up in a home of nothing but loving, supportive people. Maybe it was hubris to think she could make a difference in Lily's life with just a couple of days' friendship, but she felt the need to try nonetheless.

She expected to find a home where Lily was the Cinderella doing all the chores for a big ogre who not only barely tolerated her, but blamed her for the death of his wife. What she found was completely the opposite.

Ed was a loving father. He doted on his daughter, and it was crystal clear she set the tone for the house. Whatever she wanted, that was how it happened. It was also evident that Lily loved her father very much and doted on him just as much as he her. She cooked many of his meals, and Ed loved to sit with his eyes closed and listen to his daughter read, proud in her ability to bring the characters on the page to life in an animated way.

The soup they had for lunch was made with vegetables Lily and Serena picked from Lily's garden and venison Ed had brought down with his own claws. During grace, a practice that Serena's own family observed, she allowed Ed to take her hand. Her hand was minuscule within Ed's. She caught herself, while thanking God, wondering if Ed's hands were an indication of the size of other parts of his anatomy.

After much pleading by Lily, Serena found herself agreeing to a sleepover. In Lily's room, of course.

Marvin was a virgin. This fact had instilled in his mind feelings of inadequacy that had prevented him from pursuing to his fullest potential a healthy sex life with girls his own age or any age.

But, it was also a fact that he was now driving Marjorie up to the circus, where he had every intention of losing his virginity in one of the cast trailers that was not going to be put to a better use. And whereas he was under maximum security detail forty-eight hours previous, he was now free to roam wherever he liked with Marjorie.

So, after an obligatory stop to admire the beauty of the view, Marjorie pulled Marvin into Serena's trailer. It was a mess. It looked ransacked, thought Marvin. But, then he suspected Serena was a hippy, what with all the pills he always saw her popping. Earth children were slobs.

Marjorie brushed away the articles of clothing strewn across the little couch, lay down, and slipped off her underwear. Marvin ripped off his pants as quickly as he could, hopping around on one foot trying to remove a stuck pant leg.

He barely made it inside Marjorie before exploding.

Marvin collapsed onto Marjorie, ashamed.

"I'm so sorry. It's just that you're so beautiful. I promise. I'll be able to go again."

Marjorie giggled and tisk-tisked.

"Of course you will, silly. It's the writhing. You can't help yourself."

Marjorie devoured Marvin's lips with her mouth.

In Christopher's trailer, Jake was experiencing a very similar and equally embarrassing episode with Doreen.

"What's 'the writhing?'" Jake asked Doreen.

"When we're ready to mate, non-weres can't resist us."

Doreen looked down, between their two bodies.

"See?" she asked with a smile.

In Lily's bedroom, Lily showed Serena the watercolors she had painted and which now adorned her walls, as well as a black and white photo of her mother and father together when her mother was very pregnant with Lily.

"This is my favorite photo. It is the only photo of my mom, dad and me together," Lily said without a hint of sadness.

Lily's mother reminded Serena of her own mother. She had kind, melancholic eyes, a slender, elegant build, and a pianist's hands that wrapped across her extended belly in protective fashion.

Lily also showed Serena the tears in the Victorian fabric wallpaper, where her first turning had resulted in a redecoration of her room in what she liked to describe as abstract Lilly.

After a couple chapters of Nancy Drew over milk and a cookie split in two, it was lights out for the girls.

But Serena couldn't sleep. She was sweating profusely. It felt like a hundred degrees inside the room, her heart was beating a mile a minute, and she couldn't get the image of Ed's hands out of her brain.

Serena looked over at Lily, who was fast asleep. She got up, tiptoed to the door, slipped out, and crossed the darkened hallway to Ed's room. Serena wanted Ed to wrap himself around her and make her feel small.

Peter had no clue what had gotten into his colleagues. They had all lost their minds. Sitting around the supper table of a perfectly nice family earlier that evening had been the final straw for him.

"Do you want my daughter, lad?" The father had asked him.

The man was eager to get this show on the road.

"I'm sorry?"

"You can take her tonight. You have her mother's and my blessing."

Across from Peter, Cynthia was sipping her soup. His eye-line was continuously drawn to her breasts, which were very much apparent through the thin blouse and bra she was not wearing. He did think they were very well put together breasts, but no amount of her father prostituting his daughter was going to work on Peter.

Peter decided to just spill the beans. "I'm gay."

"That's good. Cynthia isn't of a serious disposition herself," chimed in Cynthia's mother.

Peter finished his meal quickly on that point and informed Cynthia he would return tomorrow to seal the deal.

Peter was getting the hell out of this town tonight.

Shane had an even more surreal experience. The mousy girl wasn't willing to wait. When her parents retired for the night, Zelda was prepared to take him right there on the dining room table. Shane was a meal she would top with salt and pepper. So, he decided the best way through the storm was not to avoid it.

Shane told Zelda he was modest, and she agreed to move the proceedings to her room. With the lights out, Shane was able to fumble with a condom he always kept in his wallet for emergencies.

This was going to have to work at protecting him against the ultimate in sexually transmitted diseases.

When Peter and Shane met back up at the hotel, they were both of the same mind. They escaped through the back door of the hotel and dashed from clothes line to garden shed to beat-up car until within sprinting distance of the ford in the river.

Once across it, both looked back to check they weren't being followed. Nothing. Twenty minutes later, they'd reached the circus and the vehicle that was their ticket out of here.

Shane hopped in Carter's pick-up and starting shuffling through the glove compartment and under the seats for the keys, until Peter pointed out they were in the ignition.

They closed the doors to the pick-up as quietly as they could, and Shane started up the engine, hoping that it wasn't going to be the eruption that the vehicle's age and condition suggested.

It was even louder than the young men had anticipated. Was there a muffler on this thing? Shane threw the gear shift into drive and headed down the mountain.

"I figure we've got an hour till the next town. We'll send back help from there. What's the gas situation?" Peter asked.

Shane peered down at the pump icon and saw a quarter of a tank. "I think we'll just get there or within walking distance at least."

They worked their way down the mountain road they'd first used what seemed like an eternity ago, but was in fact less than a week ago.

Wyatt and his wolves had watched Shane and Peter return to the circus. He could have easily ended their lives at any point during their escape. But, he liked to play with his prey before the kill.

Wyatt watched the truck reach the base of the mountain and come up against the pile of logs that blocked access to the rural highway. The thick forest on either side of the logjam prevented Shane and Peter from going around.

The two men jumped out and spent the next half hour trying to shift the logs. But there were too many of them. They had dislodged one of the logs through prying and pushing, but couldn't lift or roll it to one side.

"We could drag them out of the way," Peter suggested.

He ran back to the pick-up and searched through the bed until he found a jumble of rope. He tied it to the front hitch of the truck while Shane dug a trough with his hands under the log.

Shane threaded the end of the rope through to the other side and wrapped it around the log several times. He tied it off and gave Peter the thumbs-up signal.

Peter hopped in the truck, shifted into reverse and put his foot on the gas. The truck complained, but the log moved. The truck dragged the log free of the pile.

It was when dragging the second log that the rope snapped. And after tying off at a shorter distance, the rope snapped again.

Worn out and leaning against what was still a substantial pile of logs, Shane stated the obvious.

"Pete, it would take us days to move all of these. We have to make a run for it on foot."

"I know," Peter replied. "Okay."

Shane returned to the truck and grabbed a water bottle that had been rolling around on the floor, and the two men made it around the pile of logs to the entrance of the turn-off from the rural highway.

There, waiting for them, was Wyatt's pack.

CHAPTER TWENTY-TWO

At sun-up, Wyatt kicked a scrawny wolf off Peter's mutilated body. The wolf whelped, leaping forward and transforming into human Roland.

"Don't be a glutton, boy. Now, get dressed. We're going into town today."

Wyatt turned to one of his lieutenants and pointed at Peter and Shane's corpses.

"Throw what's left of them in the river."

The second night in the wilderness for Darkly and Buck was an uneventful one. Buck had not run with the moon, and she slept soundly. There was a moment when Darkly woke for an instant and sensed something walking around the tent. But, she did not feel threatened and fell asleep almost as quickly as she awoke.

Buck told her they would leave the tent where it was and merely stamp out the fire. They were a twenty-minute hike from Catharine's home. Depending on how long they stayed, they may need to camp here another night.

"Won't we stay with her?" Darkly asked.

"No." Buck was being cryptic.

Where they were situated, they were near the top of a stout mountain. The summit consisted of two craggy rock spires that resembled an old woman's arthritic fingers. Between the two spires, a bowl had been shaped in the mountain from a spring that emptied out of the bowl into the stream, which then, in turn, joined the Moon River.

It was into the bowl, the source of the spring, that Buck guided Darkly.

The floor of the bowl was a rich carpet of ferns and moss. Before the spring's water fell out of the bowl and began its long descent to the valley below, it first collected in a small pool. In the pool, there were carp. Their scales shimmered luminescent in the morning sun, and the red, orange, white, and purple colors popped against the rim of silver lichen that crowned the pool.

"I put those there for your mother. I thought it would give her something to watch."

"They're beautiful, Buck."

Darkly looked around her.

"Where's the house?"

Darkly didn't know how anyone would get building materials up here, let alone fish, but her mother, if it really was her mother, had to live somewhere.

"Let's climb up there," Buck answered.

"Okay."

Buck went first, and Darkly followed to a rock outcrop that jutted out from one of the spires. Buck sat down.

"Now what do we do?" asked Darkly.

"We wait."

Carter woke up to the warmth of the sun on his face. It felt good, but nowhere near as good as last night. He looked down at the end of the hotel bed, where a tray from room service had been placed. Well, room service is being generous. Lewis had been bribed by Mary's father with a jar of pickled onions to bring to Carter's room a bottle of Glenfiddich single malt and loaf of spiced cake.

He turned over to watch Mary sleeping, her head resting on the pillow next to his. He wasn't sure how she had captured his heart and body so quickly, and he didn't care. The urge to make love to her again was overwhelming. He wanted so badly to wake her, but she looked so peaceful.

What happens next? How does it happen? When does it come? Will it take him by surprise? He thought he should be scared about the transformation about to be thrust upon him. He thought he should be anxious about not returning home to Miami. Why was he not running for the hills like Peter and Shane? He had seen them climbing the hill across the river last night. Carter and Mary had made love twice, and he went to sit alone by the window afterwards, more content than he had ever been, while she fell asleep. That was when he saw them. He wished them well and returned to bed.

Doc Ross opened the bottle of colloidal silver pills. He sniffed them and then dumped the whole bottle down the toilet. He pulled the chain next to the cistern above his head, and the little caplets were caught up in the resulting whirlpool and disappeared. He then went to wake up Lily and tell her the heartbreaking news. Her father was dead.

He had found Ed sprawled naked on his bed, his eyes open wide as his mouth, and an erection that remained prominent after Doc covered it with a blanket.

Serena was wrapped in a blanket, crouched on the floor, rocking back and forth. When Doc read the list of ingredients on the back of the bottle he found in Serena's purse, it all became clear. Caught up in the writhing, Serena had mated with Ed. But, with her body pumped full of silver, love didn't just hurt, it killed.

Doc slapped Serena across the face to snap her out of her stupor.

"Listen to me, sweetheart," Doc lectured, "this was a simple heart attack."

He showed Serena the now empty bottle of colloidal silver.

"I've gotten rid of these. Not that anyone will ask you such an unfathomable question, but if they do, you never ingested silver, and you don't know what happened. You were both in the middle of it, when he started gasping for air. You came and got me immediately."

Doc stood up, shaking his head. He thought he'd seen it all. There really are surprises still to be had, even at his stage of life.

"There's a little girl in the next room who's crying her eyes out. She's lost her mother and her father. You're one of us now. I think you know what you need to do."

Darkly pulled an apple from her pack. It was full of worm holes, such was the organic nature of a town that considered pesticide a fancy word for scarecrow. She thought back to her childhood. She was with other children at an apple farm. She helped pick the apples, then watched them being turned into apple sauce. Wait a minute. That memory was from well before William had opened the car door and helped her into the back seat, wiping her bloodied and bare feet with a tissue.

Buck touched Darkly's arm, pulling her out of the daydream.

Below them, from a crevice in the bowl of the rock, the muzzle of a black wolf was emerging. It walked slowly onto the carpet of moss and crouched down at the carp pool, proceeding to lap up water. The wolf then settled down at the pool's edge and appeared to watch the fish swimming around the pool. The fish did not avoid the side of the pool where the wolf lounged. They appeared quite used to the company.

Buck spoke quietly to Darkly.

"The cure drove a number of children mad. There was no cure for the madness. They became violent, turning on their families. The year after Catharine came to us, nineteen children were put down."

Darkly recoiled.

"It was the only merciful option we had. To seek treatment in the outside world would have meant torture in a government lab. Your mother blamed herself, and she was right to do so. She came here, where she said goodbye to me and her infant son and swore to remain in wolf form until her death."

Had Darkly heard right? She looked down at the black wolf. Was this her mother? She looked at Buck, and he nodded his head.

"You're a bastard," Darkly said in a still rage.

"You wanted to see her. Needed to see—"

"This is either a stalling tactic designed to get me alone or you have one fucking sick sense of humor."

Buck grabbed her wrist hard.

"Ow."

"Shh."

Buck was looking over the outcrop at the wolf, who was sniffing the air in their direction. Darkly looked down into the wolf's eyes and thought she recognized them.

The wolf got up and trotted back into the crevice in the rock face.

Darkly was furious. At Buck, at herself, at the world. She ran all the way back to where she and Buck had camped the night before. Buck chased after her for a distance, but thought it best to just let her be.

Upon reaching the camp, Darkly just kept going, causing Buck to shout after her. "You won't find your way back alone."

"I'm a Mountie," Darkly yelled back. "This is what we're born for."

Buck pulled the tent stakes free, quickly bundling up the tent and kicking dirt onto the extinguished coals of the campfire. Darkly was just about out of sight, making her way down the hill, when Buck followed after her.

The custom when recruiting outsiders was that the day after the writhing, there would be a wedding or weddings before the visitors turned for the first time that night. The two wolves that ran together on the second night of mating would be husband and wife.

A wedding ceremony wasn't something that those born as werewolves bothered with. It was a construct of the outside world. But, the elders of Wolf Woods found that their recruits adapted more quickly when the niceties they were used to were adhered to in their new place of residence.

The weddings would be conducted by Reverend MacIntyre one after the other until all of the film folk were hitched. No one had seen Peter and Shane that morning, leaving two brides on the cusp of breakdowns and two fathers combing the countryside ready to deal out non-lethal thrashings.

News of Ed's untimely meeting with death was making the rounds of the town, and Serena's praises were being sung for immediately stepping up to mother Lily.

As for Carter, Jake, and Marvin, they and their brides and the brides' families were sitting down to a pancake breakfast at The Moon River Diner before walking the short distance to the church. Geraldine was in the kitchen mixing batter when she heard the bell over the diner door ring.

"How about some coffee, miss?" Wyatt asked Victoria.

"I'm afraid we're out of coffee, sir," Victoria replied coolly, though shaken by the sight of a stranger.

The voice that made it back to the kitchen was one Geraldine had not heard in seventeen years, but was recognizable in an instant.

Geraldine dropped the wooden spoon in a bowl of batter, snapped her fingers at Trey, who was bent over dirty dishes in the sink, and pointed him to the back door. Once Trey was outside, she ran to her daughter, bursting through the swing doors into the diner's dining room. She came face to face with Angie.

"This your first old lady?" asked Angie.

The newlyweds-to-be were quiet as church mice. Each one of Wyatt's pack had taken up a position at one of the diner's tables. Jake lifted his arms in the air as one of the wolves grabbed a slice of back bacon off his plate. Wyatt walked up to the table and reprimanded the man. He then grabbed him by the throat.

"Zig, now you know you've already eaten this morning. Give the man back his breakfast."

The one called Zig dropped the bacon back onto Jake's plate, and Wyatt addressed the room.

"See how order is restored when you have a proper Alpha Wolf around to set things to right?"

Wyatt looked around the room and made a display of counting the heads with his fingers.

"Then there were three. That's a shame, considering you started with six."

He looked over at Geraldine.

"Losing one is unfortunate. Three, well, that's just plain incompetent leadership. I got the low-down on this little hoe-down from a couple of nice gentlemen I met in the woods, lover."

"One's ill, in bed, on the mend," shot back Geraldine.

"Thanks to you, no doubt. On the mend, that is."

Wyatt looked in Angie's direction. She clearly didn't like him using the word "lover" in reference to anyone other than herself. Good. That would keep her on her toes.

"Three new wolves, three happy ladies," Wyatt said as he continued to scan the room. "Still, so many unsatisfied women. And I bring the men to satisfy them."

Wyatt's werewolves smiled and nodded their heads.

"Because that is what an Alpha does. He provides for the needs of his wolves."

"Go get Sheriff Buck, Victoria," ordered Geraldine.

"Nice try," Wyatt said, standing between Victoria and the door. "I know he's a couple days away from here."

Wyatt turned his attention to Victoria. He reached out and stroked her face. She slapped his hand away, and both Geraldine and Angie stepped forward. Wyatt held his hand up to stop them.

"I don't blame you. You don't know me from Adam. But, you will. You may even come to love me. But, regardless, know I love my little girl. So much so, I came back for you."

Wyatt placed his hand over his heart and then addressed the whole diner.

"For you and for your half-brother mate," Wyatt continued. Where is the little Darkly tyke, Geraldine?

"With the only father he's ever known," Geraldine lied.

Wyatt took the insult on the chin and turned to address the whole diner.

"There's a new sheriff in town, ladies and gentlemen. Accept that, and we'll all have a good time. Now, let's get you good people off to church."

The little tyke was, in fact, unlocking his father's gun cabinet and filling his own hunting rifle with silver bullets. After completing this task, which he had practiced with his father many times before, he made his way to the church to alert Doc Ross and Reverend MacIntyre, which was exactly where Wyatt and his family of werewolves were headed.

Wyatt was skipping along, joyous, singing to himself the song, *Get Me To The Church On Time*. The townsfolk at the diner followed the lunatic down the main street, where the singing stopped, and Wyatt called a halt to the wedding parties.

Standing in front of them, in the middle of the street next to the church, was Trey. His rifle was pointed straight at Wyatt's head. Wyatt's men turned and stood in front of Wyatt, protecting him, Angie and their son, Roland. The royal family.

"Shh," Wyatt said, as he stroked one of the wolves on the back and stepped towards Trey.

Trey slipped the safety off his rifle. His hand was shaking. He had never seen anything like this before. Wyatt was able to control the wolves while in human form. They actually responded to him and did as he commanded.

"Now, boy," Wyatt said calmly, "I'm not here to cause pain and suffering. I'm here to ask you all to welcome a long-lost son home again."

"Then why didn't you wait to show up when the sheriff was around?" Trey asked.

"Ha ha," Wyatt wagged his finger. "Smart kid."

At that moment, Doc Ross and Reverend MacIntyre rushed out the church doors and stopped at the steps leading down to the street.

"Wyatt," whispered the Reverend to himself.

"Morning, vicar!" Wyatt called out to the Reverend in a forced English accent.

Wyatt took a couple of steps forward toward Trey to test the waters. The boy did not hold his ground, Wyatt noted. He backed up. Trey would collapse under pressure.

"Come inside, Trey," Doc Ross called out.

"No, Trey. Just hear me out here, son," Wyatt said, while moving a couple more steps closer to the boy. "Just hear me out. I've been watching things in Wolf Woods from a distance. How many children did you see buried under my brother's watch? How many wore the very instrument of our torture around their necks? He even put it on you, son. Why? Because he hates what he is. He hates what we all are by the Grace of God."

Wyatt glanced in Reverend MacIntyre's direction.

"He hates what God made us, and he hates what you are."

"No. My father's a good man. Everyone knows that."

"Your father? No, Trey, I'm your father. My brother banished me and then banished your mother, but held on to you to secure the position he had not earned."

Trey moved his finger closer to the trigger.

"Son, I'm not here to take anything away from you. I'm here to restore what is yours. Yours because of me. No one should have taken that right from you. The right to challenge me when the time comes and take up your duties as Alpha of this town. A town that is healthy and prosperous."

Shit, thought Geraldine, Trey was wavering. Wyatt was getting to him. Better to shoot Wyatt and leave his wolves without a leader.

"I'm not going to hurt Buck, son. He's my brother. Despite all that has passed between us, we're blood. He and I will talk this out. What matters is you. I've come back to a place of suffering because I've figured out the solution. It's you. And I know in the very heart of my being that only your true father can help you realize your destiny, and then you, Victoria, and your children will bring this town back from the dead. If Buck truly cares about what's best for you, he'll hear me out."

Geraldine wanted to shout it out, reveal the truth once and for all that Trey was not Wyatt's son. As charming a werewolf as he was, he could be damn stupid, and sure as hell couldn't count. In this instance, that worked to his benefit. It was his sheer bravado that allowed Wyatt's twelve wolves to take on a town of almost three hundred. But, boy, did she want to see the look on Wyatt's face when she called him a fool. A meaty baby boy had been born only seven months after the rape. That boy was no more Wyatt's son than Buck's.

But, Geraldine knew she'd be torn to shreds before the last words were out of her mouth. So, she watched helpless as Trey lowered his rifle and Wyatt placed an arm over Trey's shoulder.

"Now," Wyatt said, "Let's go into the church."

Wyatt looked back to see his naked werewolves standing over their ripped clothes.

"You lot stay outside. You aren't dressed for a wedding."

CHAPTER TWENTY-THREE

Darkly and Buck made it back to the canoe in silence. Moving downhill all day meant their return time would be cut drastically. They'd paddle till the sun was a half hour from setting, then make camp along the river's bank.

Darkly scanned the trees on the riverbank. She had the strangest feeling they were being followed, but could see nothing to prove it. If Buck felt the same, he didn't mention it.

They were given even more impetus to hurry when Darkly spotted floating ahead of them, two bodies. Buck reached out and pulled one of the bodies next to the canoe.

"You may want to avert your eyes," Buck said.

"I'm an RCMP Constable. I've seen dead people before," Darkly replied.

That was the most they had spoken to each other in hours. The body they pulled close was barely recognizable. But, barely is a far cry from not at all in the world of police investigation.

"How about people that have been half eaten?" asked Buck.

Darkly recognized panic in that implacable voice.

"It's Peter. Who did this?"

"Someone's taken advantage of my absence," Buck suggested, as he began to paddle harder. "My son's in danger."

Darkly paddled with all her might. Now, they would paddle through the night. Everything that happened between Buck and her that morning was forgiven.

Wyatt kept a low profile during the wedding proceedings and celebrations. He didn't want to alarm the natives. The best way to deal with the situation was to just allow them to get used to him. Once that was the norm, then he'd crack the whip.

Wyatt took Buck's keys off Trey and toured his new office, putting his feet up on the desk, testing the strength of the jail cell bars, and pouring over Buck's notes.

It was in those notes that Wyatt learned the town of Wolf Woods was playing host to two Mounties. He also learned of Geraldine's pitiful attempt at murder. Wyatt reached into Buck's, now his, desk drawer and pulled out Gus's RCMP badge.

Wyatt had instructed Geraldine to miss the festivities and to wait at the diner for him. They were long due a catch-up. Wyatt walked in alone this time. He sat down at the diner counter, and Geraldine pulled out a bottle of homemade whisky from a cupboard and poured a glass each for her and Wyatt. Wyatt downed his in one gulp.

"Gerri, why did you try to kill the male constable?"

"Why do you think, Wyatt?"

"Well, I know what you would say to anyone else. You'd say he was a threat to the safety of the entire town. If Buck wasn't going to deal with it, well then, you would."

Geraldine poured Wyatt another shot.

"Sounds like the right reason to me, Wyatt."

Geraldine downed her first whisky while Wyatt downed his second.

"I'm not anyone else," Wyatt said, pushing his glass towards Geraldine for a third shot. "I think you can't abide competition, oh love of my life. I think you thought if you try to kill one of them, then the other will come out guns blazing, and then Buck has to kill the pretty girl."

Wyatt grabbed the bottle and poured himself the third shot and poured Geraldine her second.

"Drink up. It will put you in the mood."

"For what, Wyatt? After all these years, you can't tell me you still feel something? Besides, you found yourself a younger model."

Wyatt smiled and pushed Geraldine's glass towards her. He then placed, next to the shot, Gus's badge.

"I said drink up."

Geraldine did as she was told. Wyatt hopped off his stool and went to the door and held it open.

"Ladies first," he said.

Geraldine had no clue where this was going. Wyatt wouldn't kill her right away. He was more calculating than that. He'd wait until things calmed down. She knew him that well at least. Or had the psychopath changed?

Wyatt escorted Geraldine to Doc Ross's place. Gus was well enough that he didn't need around the clock care. Feeling had even returned to his legs. With Doc and Mrs. Ross at the nuptials, Gus was on his own. Wyatt opened the unlocked door to the house and held his hand out for Geraldine to enter.

"What are we doing here, Wyatt?" Geraldine asked.

"Trust me, Gerri."

"Never."

But, Geraldine knew she had no choice in the matter. So, despite her words, she entered the house and climbed the steps up to Gus's room. She and Wyatt didn't enter right away.

"You see, I think you didn't mean for the brave constable to get hurt. At least not as bad as he was. I think you underestimated the power of an adolescent wolf and how distracted Buck could become when he's finally met *the one*."

Wyatt let those words sink in and then leaned in close to Geraldine.

"Have you forgotten how I used to fuck you when we were thirteen?"

Geraldine felt herself go flush. She reached out and grabbed Wyatt's belt, but he removed her hands.

"Like you pointed out, I'm with a younger model now. As for Gus in there, if you really want him dead, now's your chance. Protect the town. Or perhaps there's another way to skin a man."

Wyatt knocked on the door.

"Hello?" Gus called out.

Wyatt whispered the rest to Geraldine.

"Either they carry a dead man out of there, or a wolf walks out on his own accord tonight."

Wyatt stepped aside, and Geraldine walked through the door not knowing yet what choice she was going to make.

She closed the door behind her and slipped off her cardigan. Wyatt's closeness had awaken something in her, and she was feeling warm. Gus, on the other hand, was feeling downright cold.

"What the fuck are you doing in here? You think you're going to apologize?" Gus practically shouted at her.

"Yes," Geraldine responded simply, and began undressing. She had decided.

"Whoa, what are you doing?"

Geraldine pulled back the covers to the bed. She sat on the edge, lifted Gus's t-shirt and kissed his stomach.

"Stop," commanded Gus.

But Geraldine didn't stop. She moved farther south, pulling Gus's shorts down, revealing him. Gus tried to shift his body, but he was still too weak.

Geraldine took note of the healing scars on the leg that had been a wolf's meal, and she finally spoke.

"I'm going to make these wounds disappear."

Wyatt heard Gus gasp from outside the door. The protests quickly gave way to moans, as the writhing overtook him. Wyatt bent down to look through the keyhole and watched as Geraldine mounted the constable and guided him into her.

Geraldine looked back at the door. She knew Wyatt would be watching. He always had been both an exhibitionist and a voyeur.

The brides would be with their husbands to turn with them their first time, to hold their hand for as long as that was possible. Once a ray of the moon hit their skin, it was game on. In truth, now that they had mated, they would rarely take up a moon run apart.

Serena and Lily, mother and daughter, would run together. And Geraldine would run with the man she tried to kill. If only healing those who had taken the cure could be as easy as what she did for Gus. But, there was a price to pay. Geraldine understood that because they had mated in human form and would run together as wolves, it was inevitable they would become tied together on a level Gus couldn't comprehend lying in the middle of a field outside of town. It would be difficult at first for them both to accept, but they would have to come to terms with it in time.

Marvin's wife had learned how to turn at any moment. As a child, she first turned in the schoolroom at the age of six. She had been so embarrassed afterwards. But for Marvin, a convert, it must be the touch of the moon that initiates the transformation on the first nightfall after consummation. So, Marjorie took him by the hand and walked him naked into the moonlight.

All were naked. It was Carter who helped Mary, lifting her up into his arms and marching proudly into the light. Then Jake, then Serena, then Gus, lying on the grass, his hand gripped tightly by Geraldine's, felt the heat of moonlight on their faces. And their lives were changed forever.

Buck and Darkly dragged the canoe up towards the old mine, behind the rock outcrop.

"We can't just walk into town. We need to get a look at what's been going on first."

Buck reached into his pack and pulled out his and Darkly's gun. He handed Darkly her gun.

"Here."

"You didn't think of giving it back before now?" Darkly asked, incredulous.

"You didn't need it where we were going," replied Buck, "and now you might."

Buck forged ahead, and Darkly pulled him back.

"Hey, macho man. I don't have time to deliver a lesson on sexism just now. But, I'm willing to bet the RCMP firing range made me a helluva lot better shot than the tin cans you grew up throwing rocks at. I'll take point."

Darkly took the lead moving up the hill, and it wasn't long before they reached the movie's circus. Darkly and Buck searched the cast trailers.

"They've been turned upside down," said Darkly.

"And the truck's gone," Buck noted.

"Maybe some of my people got away," Darkly said.

They made their way to the railing of the overlook. Each removed a pair of binoculars from their packs and scanned the town.

"Looks peaceful enough," said Darkly.

Buck moved his binoculars up to the field above town. There, he spotted the newlyweds turning from human to wolf.

"Geraldine," he said aloud, incredulous.

"What?" asked Darkly.

"Your people are now my people," Buck responded.

Darkly watched through her own binoculars as Gus leapt up off the ground a whole and powerful wolf, while Buck lowered the binoculars back down to town and The Blue Moon Diner. Outside the front door of the diner, Wyatt was waving at him.

"If I have any people. Shit."

Darkly also focused her sights on Wyatt and lost her breath. Waving back at her was the man she had tasted all those years ago in Algonquin Park.

"Throw your weapons over here," the voice behind Buck and Darkly ordered.

Buck and Darkly turned slowly to see Zig standing over them, a rifle pointed between their two heads.

"In case you're wondering, Buck, I'm packing silver bullets. It is Buck, right? You match the description."

"That's me," Buck confirmed.

"And this must be the Mountie? I'm going to enjoy this. I always hated you people. Seeing as Wyatt's brother likes you so much, I'm to kill you. Wyatt prefers to do the honors with you, Buck."

Zig moved the rifle directly in front of Darkly's head. "Bye bye."

Darkly did not freeze when confronted with her own demise. If she was going down, she was going down in an offensive stance. But, as she leapt forward, Buck valiantly dived in front of Darkly, resulting in an outcome reminiscent of an American football tackle.

In the fractions of a second between Darkly and Buck's mash-up and Zig repositioning his rifle's aim, a black wolf flew out of the darkness behind Zig and tackled him to the ground. He barely had time to scream, as the wolf tore into Zig's neck, separating his head from his body. His head rolled away before the rifle barrel hit the ground.

But when it did hit, the rifle discharged a bullet into the black wolf. The wolf stumbled and collapsed in a God-awful yelp.

Darkly expected to be dead seconds earlier. The shock of what just happened seeped in. The wolf that saved Darkly's life licked at its chest, and Buck went to the beast immediately.

"She's seriously wounded," Buck said.

"She?" asked Darkly.

Buck nodded his head. He crouched down and ran his hands across the top of her head. Darkly held back. The wolf looked up at her and whimpered.

"Is she going to make it?" Darkly asked.

"The bullet was a silver bullet," was all Buck said in reply.

Darkly looked over at Zig's decapitated body, and the magnitude of what had just happened sunk in. The attack was calculated, protective. Darkly looked down at the wolf that Buck would have her believe was her mother. What if she was her mother?

Darkly sat down next to Buck and took the wolf's head, placing it in her lap. She stroked the wolf's chin, as the animal continued to look up at Darkly. The whimpers turned quiet, and the wolf's breathing labored until it lost consciousness.

The wolf's blood-soaked chest continued to expand and collapse, but the movements became gestures of ever-increasing importance. The labored intakes of air gave way to the hiss of life lost. Darkly felt the final release of breath on her face.

Darkly buried her head in Buck's embrace. He said nothing and simply held her. When she looked back, the wolf's head in her lap had, after many years of exile, changed back to that of her mother, Catharine. Catharine, the wolf, had somehow recognized her and followed her back to Wolf Woods. Perhaps Buck expected that very thing to happen.

Darkly bent over and pressed her cheek next to her mother's, wishing she could never let go. The memories of her childhood came flooding back.

CHAPTER TWENTY-FOUR

Buck could only give Darkly so much time to grieve. He persuaded her to allow him to bury Catharine's body, properly, in the cemetery where Catharine's own parents were buried. But not tonight.

So, they hid Catharine unceremoniously under a pile of leaves, and Buck prepared to say goodbye to Darkly forever.

"That shot that killed your mother. Wyatt will think that is you under the leaves. He will think everything is going according to plan. I have to go down there and face him now."

"I can help," Darkly said, believing it.

"No, you can't. This isn't your fight."

"Gus—"

"Gus is my cousin now. You can damn sure bet I'll be keeping a man of his skills close. That goes for all the new…"

"Werewolves," Darkly finished Buck's thought.

"They're all my kin now. You don't have to worry about any of them. I promise you they'll be happy. So will your brother. Now, you need to leave. Or Wyatt will find a way to use you and that cure of yours to turn the town against me. If he hasn't already. He's a very persuasive sociopath. You stay, I lose."

Darkly stood in silence, plotting a leap over the railing. Buck would follow and chastise her later while they were mopping up the mess. She wanted revenge. She could taste the death *she* was about to deal out.

"I know you think you can help, and there's no one I'd rather have by my side for what lies ahead. This is bad. But, you'll only make things worse. Go."

Darkly had not run from a fight before, and maybe her emotional state was compromised, but she could not deny Buck was right about this one. She had been trained to exercise control in the most harried of circumstances. Darkly saw the truth through the haze of her quiet rage. She put common sense to use, grabbed her pack, and began walking away. Then, she ran back to Buck, grabbed his face, and kissed him deeply.

Buck opened his mouth to speak, but Darkly silenced him.

"I know," she said.

"I was about to say, 'Would you just go!'"

Darkly left. Now it was Buck's turn.

"Darkly Stewart," he called.

Darkly didn't take the bait. She just kept walking down in the direction of the highway.

"If you ever find yourself in the woods and think a wolf is tracking you, you're probably right."

Darkly smiled through the tears and turned to see a wolf leaping over the guard rail.

Darkly made it to the rural highway, and then to the Trans-Canada Highway, where she hitched a lift to Prince Rupert.

Whether Buck had saved the day or just bought her time, no wolf had caught up to her. She found her way to the Greyhound Station, where instead of hopping a bus back east, she decided to explore some old memories. She bought a ticket to Portland, Oregon.

Just north of the U.S.-Canadian border, the bus pulled over at a rest stop. Darkly had been on the bus for twelve hours and needed to wash up. She stepped into the small women's room and locked the door.

Darkly removed the scarf from around her neck and ran her fingers along the blue spider webs and the moon pendant that produced them. She thought about Buck, about Trey, about Gus and Geraldine. What would become of them? Had she done the right thing in leaving them behind?

Darkly wrapped her hand around the moon pendant, gripping it tightly.

"What if?" she asked herself.

Darkly Stewart pulled at the necklace until the silver chain snapped, and the moon pendant fell away.

THE END...until...

DARKLY STEWART: LIGHT AND DARKLY

Hellbent on revenge, Darkly returns to Wolf Woods, where evil forces have taken hold, and young children are being stolen away from their families. Darkly comes up against a local superstition her fellow Mounties have had run-ins with before... a creature that lives deep in the woods and is far darker of spirit than werewolves.

Nebuchanezzar clawed his way through the red dirt with hands he had not used in more years than he could recall. This was a man dragging himself back from the wilderness. A man reborn. He reached the stream's edge and looked down at the moving reflection, startling himself. Nebuchanezzar vomited. The haze in his mind was clearing, but his natural visage was alien and unnatural to behold.

The young wolves had followed him to the stream, whimpering from a lack of comprehension at the transformation that was taking place. Their fear surpassed their curiosity when the Angel of the Lord descended upon Nebuchanezzar, and the wolves retreated into the cover of brush.

The Angel's feet slipped through the water, and ripples washed over Nebuchanezzar. He waited for death.

But, the Angel of the Lord lifted Nebuchanezzar to his feet and said, "You are a beast no more. Stand as a man stands."

Nebuchanezzar's naked body shook from the cold. So, the Angel commanded him to sit and called the wolves to the man's side. They came, unafraid, for the Angel of the Lord wished them to be so. The beasts wrapped themselves around the man and warmed him.

"You are redeemed, Nebuchanezzar," proclaimed the Angel. "Let your children of the wilderness be a constant reminder to you and your descendants of past sins."

Then, the Angel of the Lord became like the water he stood in, maintaining his shape for a split second, before collapsing into the stream.

There was that taste. It reminded Darkly of pressing the tip of her tongue to a battery. The man appeared benign enough. Middle-aged, he wore an immaculate suit, and his expression revealed neither impatience nor a carefree nature. Darkly thought he looked like a CEO. Where was it that she read four percent of all CEOs were sociopaths?

Threat to society or not, this man standing in front of her at the post office had killed someone not that long ago. Was it a relative's suffering he brought to an end with an overdose of morphine? Or had this man recently fulfilled a taboo desire?

Darkly took a swig of the diet coke in her hand and shook it off. She looked down at the postcard of a vineyard in the Okanagan Valley and turned it over. The ends of her hair dripped due to the rain outside from which she had just escaped, and the ink was a little smudged as a result. But the message was still legible. *I'm safe. Don't worry. You'll see me again. Love, Darkly.*

Darkly thanked the trucker and climbed down from the cab. She'd found him in a diner on the outskirts of Vancouver, where she binged on complex carbs and proteins after flashing her RCMP badge and joining him in his booth. She had to get herself as far away as possible from any populated area, and Darkly didn't know when she would next eat a full meal. Would she feed when she turned? Would the need to hunt take hold instinctually?

At this moment, she listened to his eighteen-wheeler shift gears as it disappeared in a bend of the road up ahead. She was alone and as ready as she'd ever be.

Darkly estimated she was thirty miles from Wolf Woods. Maybe a little less. The rain had not stopped pouring on the drive north, and Darkly pulled her water-proof hood tightly around her head as she left the road for the cover of the pine woods. Tonight, she would camp a few yards from the road, and then follow the highway for most of the next day. She knew how much ground an animal the size of a wolf could cover in a night. But she would not confront Wyatt until she knew the facts about herself. She would face those facts alone in the woods, and then she would kill the man responsible for the death of her family.

THE AUTHOR

DG Wood lives in Los Angeles with his wife, daughter, and little werewolf. He is a screenwriter and novelist, as well as a voting member of the British Academy of Film and Television Arts.

Printed in Great
Britain
by Amazon